Books By Donna Schwa.

The Trident Trilogy

Eight Years

The Only Reason

Wild Card

The Grand Slam Series

Truth or Tequila

Raine Out

Leave It On The Field

The Blitzen Bay Series

The Runaway Bride of Blitzen Bay

No One Wants That

Pretty Close To Perfect - Preorder on Amazon.

TRUTH OR TEQUILA
(The Grand Slam Series: Book One)

DONNA SCHWARTZE

This book is a work of fiction. Names, places, characters, organizations, events, and incidents are either products of the author's imagination or are used fictitiously. Any resemblance to actual persons, living or dead, or to businesses, companies, events, institutions, or locales is completely coincidental. Any trademarks, product names, service marks, and named features are assumed to be the property of their respective owners and are only used for references. This book is intended for adults only due to sensitive language and sexual content.

ISBN: 9798544771241

Published by Donna Schwartze, 2021

donnaschwartzeauthor@gmail.com

❀ Created with Vellum

TRUTH OR TEQUILA

(The Grand Slam Series: Book One)

DONNA SCHWARTZE

For the friends who always have our backs.

"One tequila, two tequila, three tequila, floor."
— George Carlin

Chapter One

SOPHIE

"We're not changing bars because she's late!" Savannah screams as Maisie scans her phone around the packed bar so I can see what I'm up against.

Savannah planned Maisie's bachelorette party. She chose the most hellish bar in South Beach. It only holds about two hundred people. On an average night, it's hard to get in. When a celebrity shows up, it's impossible.

"It looks crazier than usual. What's going on?" I glance at my phone as I try to switch lanes on the causeway again. Traffic's crawling. So far, I've seen two wrecks and a stalled car.

Maisie points the phone at herself. She's wearing a crown with white, blinking lights surrounding the word "Bride" and a sash that says "Mrs. Right" in gold, glittery letters.

"I don't know. We're sitting right below the VIP area. Security's getting tight. There must be someone big headed this way. Van, do you see anyone yet?"

She turns the phone back to Savannah who's standing on

her chair, craning her neck to see into the upper deck. She's wearing the brightest orange dress I've ever seen. She looks a little like a traffic cone.

"No one yet," she says, suddenly looking down at the phone and pointing, "but I intend to stay here to find out even if you can't get in, Sophia. It's not our fault you're always late."

"Why do you keep inviting her, Maisie?" I whine. "You know I can only take her in small doses."

"Soph," Maisie says, laughing. "She planned the bachelorette party. She's in the wedding."

"Oh, she doesn't want me here now?" Savannah's six feet away from the phone, but she's louder than Maisie. "At least I'm on time for our best friend's bachelorette party."

Maisie and I have been best friends since we were five. We've known Savannah since college. Maisie likes her, and that's the only reason I tolerate her.

"Maisie, you know she only does this to get attention." Savannah's still yelling. "She's going to be late for your wedding so she can steal that spotlight, too."

Actually, I hate the spotlight. I'm kind of an introvert. If I ever get married, it will be a small, private ceremony, and I'm not having a bachelorette party.

"I won't be late to the wedding, Mae."

"I know, sweetie." Maisie points the camera at herself again. "But only because I'll make you stay in the hotel with me the night before."

"Soph." Maisie turns the phone to Serena, one of our other college friends. "The guy at the next table said they stopped letting people in a few minutes ago. You might not get in."

"I'll get in." I maneuver around another car. "I've finally made it off the bridge. I'll be there in twenty tops."

"She's not going to get in!" Savannah screeches. I'm sure the people sitting at the next table want to kill her. "And I'm not leaving here!"

"Savannah!" Maisie yells and then lowers her voice. "First, quit yelling. My God, why are you always so loud? And second, Sophie will get in. Settle down."

"How's she going to get in?" Savannah's voice has gotten a little bit quieter but not any less bitchy.

"Have you ever looked at her? She never has a problem getting in anywhere," Maisie snarls.

"Mae, I just turned onto Collins. I'll see you in a few."

"Okay. Be careful, Soph."

I throw my phone on the dashboard as I weave through a few cars. My friend Roman owns a little boutique hotel on the beach. He lets me park in his spot when he's not in town. It's a few blocks away from the bar, but I think it will be faster to run the rest of the way. I swerve into his hotel's parking lot.

"Ma'am, our lot's closed!" The hotel's parking attendant runs toward my car as I drive around the "Lot Full" sign.

"Hey." I smile as I lower my window. "Roman Garcia lets me park in his spot when he's not in town."

He raises his eyebrows. "Roman Garcia? Like the man who owns this hotel?"

"Yeah." I can tell he doesn't believe me. I've never seen him before. He must be new. "Hold up. Let me call him."

"Ma'am, I need you to clear the driveway." He hits the roof of my car a few times.

I ignore him as I dial Roman. It rings a few times before he picks up.

"Sophia!" Roman doesn't use FaceTime much. As usual, he's holding the phone way too close. All I can see are his eyes and part of his forehead.

"Hey, Roman. Can I use your spot at the hotel tonight? It's crazy down here and I'm so late."

Roman's one of my former clients. I helped his hotel recover from an onslaught of bad press resulting from a food poisoning incident. He's my biggest fan now and he's become one of my best friends.

"You're late? That's shocking, Soph," he says, laughing. "And you know you can always use that spot, honey. Henry knows to let you in."

"There's somebody new." I turn the camera toward the lot attendant who's pushing my car—like he's going to move it or something.

"Hey." Roman drags out his greeting as he tries to figure out who's working the lot. I hold the phone closer to the attendant. "Oh, it's Orlando. Hey man, it's Roman. Let Sophia use my spot any time she needs it."

Orlando leans into the phone. "Oh. Okay. Yes, sir," he says, stepping quickly out of the way. He runs ahead of me and removes the chain blocking Roman's spot.

"Thanks, Rome." I turn the camera back toward me. "Hey, did you get a call from Gary Randall for a reference?"

"Yeah, yesterday," he grunts. "I gave you a glowing review, of course, but I told him how direct you are. Gary's not as laid back as I am. He's kind of an asshole."

4

"Well, I have a meet-and-greet with him tomorrow, so I guess he's okay with my directness. You know their current situation. The media's been talking about nothing else. He needs me."

"Yeah, he does need you. Just watch out for him. I think he's more interested in covering up scandal, than facing it and getting better. He's not very evolved. Scratch that. He's not at all evolved. And then there's his son, Gentry. All kinds of rumors about him."

"What kind of rumors?" I say, refreshing my lipstick in the rearview mirror.

"Not good ones. He's a spoiled brat. I think he's used to taking what he wants—whether or not it wants to be taken, if you know what I mean. Just be careful. Don't be alone with him until you get a better read."

"Noted." I focus the phone on my face. "Does this lipstick do anything for me? It's new."

"Yeah, honey. It's beautiful." He tilts his head. "Your hair looks a little questionable. It's stuck to the side of your head. When's the last time you washed it?"

"This morning," I sigh, as I try to fluff it with my fingers. "It's so humid here today."

"Maybe put it up. What are you wearing?"

"That white, flowy maxi dress you like. You know the one you said I should only wear running through lilac fields in Provence."

"The see-through one?" His eyebrows furrow. "Are you wearing something under it this time?"

"It's not see-through," I say, scanning the phone down my body. "Do you think hair up is okay with this?"

"All I'm seeing is your cleavage. Get out of the car and give me a full body shot."

Orlando looks at me suspiciously from across the lot as I prop the phone up on the roof of my car and do a few spins for Roman.

"First, it's definitely see-through, and second, hair up is perfect. Maybe a low side ponytail coming over your shoulder."

I grab a tie out of my bag and use my window as a mirror. "Better?" I say, turning back to the phone.

"Much. Pull that top part up a little. Yeah, like that. Sexy as hell."

"Who's sexy as hell?" I hear Michael, Roman's husband, laughing in the background. Roman turns the phone around to him.

"Momma mia, Sophia!" Michael clasps his hand over his chest. "You're going to turn me with that little dress you're wearing. Your boobies look beautiful."

"What do you know about boobs?" Roman's rolling his eyes as he turns the phone back to himself.

"I know they're pretty to look at—"

"Look, but not touch," Roman laughs.

"No, I don't want to touch." Michael walks into the picture and scrunches his face up.

Roman shakes his head and sighs. "Soph, will you please come to the island with us next time? There are too many gays down here for me?"

"Honey, you're gay."

"I know, but I need a little straight to balance the energy. You can bring Sam."

I grimace. Roman and Michael are crazy protective of me. I've been avoiding telling them. "I broke up with Sam."

"What?" they say in unison as Roman puts the phone right up to his face. His chin is tight. I can tell he's clenching his teeth.

"What happened, Soph? Did he do something to you?" Roman growls. His eyes are narrowing into his scary look. I've literally seen grown men cry when he's looked at them like this. "I'm calling Los. He and the guys can pay Sam a little visit while we're out of town."

"Keep your crazy brothers away from him!" I try unsuccessfully to stare him down. "Roman! I'm serious. It's a long story, but it's a good thing that I'm rid of him. Everyone needs to forget about him and move on. Promise me."

"Do I need to call Maisie to get the story?"

"Excuse me?" I spritz rose water on my face to try to cool down. "Maisie's been my best friend since we were kids. She's loyal to me, not you."

"You know how much she loves me—"

"Roman!" I point into the phone and try to give him my fiercest look. "Back off!"

He stares at me for a minute. "Okay," he says slowly, "but if I find out he—"

"Stop!" I take a deep breath. "Forget about it, please. I've got to go. I'm already so late. Maisie's going to kill me. It's her bachelorette."

"Aww, tell her congrats for us," Michael says as he starts massaging Roman's shoulders. "And promise us you won't get too drunk, Little Miss Lightweight."

"I promise. I have a morning meeting. I'm probably not going to drink tonight."

"Famous last words." Michael gets right up next to the phone and blows me a kiss.

"Bye, guys. Love you!"

As I hang up, I hear Michael yelling, "Bye, Sophia. You're too good for Sam. You're too good for everyone."

Chapter Two

SEB

"Seb! Seb!"

When I get out of my car, all I see are cell phones pointed at me. I can't go anywhere in this town without people shoving their phones in my face. I know it's part of being a professional baseball player. I'm not complaining. I love my job. I just wish it didn't come with so much fame.

"Hey." I give a halfhearted wave to the crowd that's gathered in front of the hotel. Everyone knows the hotel's bar is the biggest celebrity hangout in town. There's always a line waiting to get in, but it's crazier than usual tonight. There must be a hundred people crowding the sidewalk in front.

"Are you going to sign an autograph?" Joe says, clearing a path for me. The team requires me to have full-time security. Joe's my guy. He's a former Marine. Most of the time, he acts like he's still at war.

"Damn, Joe. How many guys do you have here tonight?" I say as some of the team's other security guys swarm around me. I hate having a security detail. I know they're only doing their jobs—protect the "franchise." That's what the media labeled me after I signed the largest contract in baseball history. Since I signed, the team's owners treat me like I'm made of glass. I know they don't want me to get hurt, but damn, I'm six foot three, 210 pounds. I can pretty much look after myself.

The crowd's screaming for autographs and selfies. I rarely do either anymore. When I was a rookie, I'd stand on rope lines and sign autographs for hours, but now—eight years into my major league career—I only sign for kids. One of the local sports blogs reported that fact, so now I have to be on the lookout for people using kids to get my autograph for themselves.

Sports memorabilia dealers hire kids to stand in line to get my autograph, then take it from them, and sell it online. As crazy as that is, they're not even the worst. Women use their kids to lure me in, then try to slip me their numbers or their hotel room keys. I usually ignore them, but a few years back, my curiosity got the best of me. I asked a woman what she planned to do with her kid if we went back to her hotel room. She said he could wait outside in the hallway. He was like five years old. The media calls me jaded. Yeah, I wonder why.

I finally see the kid who's going to get the only autograph of the night. She's about five years old. She's standing over to the side, holding her dad's hand and pressed firmly against his leg. I can tell she hates crowds as much as I do. She's wearing my jersey like a dress. It falls well below her knees. She must wear it a lot because it's really faded. When I smile at her, she smiles and quickly buries her face in her dad's leg. Security holds the crowd back as I squat down to talk to her.

"Hey." I tilt my head to try to see her around her dad's leg. She peeks out, sees me, and buries her face in his leg again. "Hey, I don't bite. Well, most of the time anyway."

I growl a little bit and chomp my teeth. She giggles and looks up at me—still holding onto her dad's hand for dear life.

"What's your name? My name's Seb." I hold my hand out to her.

"Belle," she whispers as she puts her tiny hand into mine.

"That's a pretty name." I shake her hand gently. "That's the name of the lady in *Beauty and the Beast*, right?"

She nods her head emphatically.

"Is that your favorite Disney movie?"

She pushes away from her dad's leg but keeps hold of his hand. "No, I like *Frozen* better. Do you like Disney movies?"

"I love Disney movies. *Aladdin* is my favorite, but it's kind of an old one. Have you seen it?"

Her brow furrows as she tries to remember. "I don't think so."

"I'll make you a deal," I say, holding my hand up to Joe. He hands me a Sharpie. "I'll sign your jersey if you promise you'll watch *Aladdin*."

She looks up at her dad—not sure if she can make the promise by herself. He nods and smiles at her. "We can watch *Aladdin*. I like that one, too."

She looks back at me and holds out her hand. "Deal."

I shake her hand again. "Turn around. I'll sign the back. Do you spell your name B-e-l-l-e?"

Her dad says, "Yes," from above us.

To Belle -
We made a deal.
Seb Miller #20

I look at the dad. "You want a picture of us?"

"Yeah, if it wouldn't be too much of an imposition. She loves you."

I nod as Belle turns back around. "Belle, is it okay if I get my picture taken with you?"

"It's okay, Seb." She smiles as she dives into my arms like we're best friends now. I lift her and take a step back so her dad can get the shot. She lays her head on my shoulder when her dad tells her to smile. My heart melts and drips all the way down to my toes. I give her a little squeeze before I hand her back to her dad.

"Hey, thanks for being so nice to her." The dad shakes my hand. "She'll remember this forever."

"So will I. She's a good kid." I hold up my hand for a high-five which she enthusiastically gives me. "It was nice meeting you, Belle. Will you write to me and tell me how you liked *Aladdin*?"

She nods again—this time flashing a wide grin. I smile, tap Joe, and point at the dad. Joe hands him a card with the P.O. Box address for my special fan mail—the stuff that gets answered.

As I walk up the stairs to the entrance, I turn back around

to give the crowd one more obligatory wave. For some reason, my eyes go to a woman typing frantically on her phone. She's the only one in the crowd who's not looking at me. I'm immediately turned on by that.

As I take a closer look, I see a lot of other things that turn me on. The sun's setting behind her—outlining what looks like a beautiful body under her sheer dress. She has her sunglasses hanging from the front of the dress. They're causing the already low neckline to dip even farther, exposing gentle, ample curves. Her long hair's in a ponytail that's coming over one shoulder. I'd like to see it free, falling over her tanned, toned arms. In fact, I'd like to see everything falling tonight—the hair, the dress, and anything she might or might not be wearing underneath.

She looks up at the sky and lets out a long breath—like she's trying to calm herself down. She glances at her phone again and then looks toward the stairs. She sees me staring at her and rolls her eyes. She has absolutely no interest in me. I'm not even sure she knows who I am. God, could she get any more perfect?

"That one," I say to Joe, nodding my head toward her. "The blonde with the long, white dress. Make sure she gets in."

"Yep," he says as he pushes me into the bar.

Chapter Three

SOPHIE

"That one—right there. Let her in." A stout man, wearing all black, is pointing at me. His lips are tight, and his eyes are squinted into slits. He's pissed about something.

One of the hotel security guys unhooks the barrier rope, grabs my elbow, and pulls me through. He pushes me toward the man in black.

"I'm Joe. My client wants you let into the bar," he says, not looking at me. He's reading something on his phone.

"Hi Joe. Who's your client? The guy who just walked in? Honestly, I have no idea who he is."

"Yeah, I'm sure that's why he noticed you." Joe looks up at me briefly and then looks back down at his phone. He has no interest in me, except as a potential conquest for his client. I'm guessing Joe plays pimp for him all of the time.

"Uh, just so we're on the same page, I have absolutely no interest in meeting your boy."

He laughs and finally focuses on me. "How do you know my boy has any interest in meeting you?"

I stare at him for a second. "Look, I'm beyond late for my best friend's bachelorette party, so I appreciate you getting me in, but if there are strings attached, I'd rather stay out here."

"No strings," he says, motioning me to go ahead of him. "I'd prefer you stay away from my client. He doesn't need the distraction right now, and you're just his type."

"Oh, yeah? What's his type?" I say, rolling my eyes. "Women who are oblivious to him?"

"Exactly. And all this doesn't hurt." He waves his hand up and down my body. "Promise me you'll ignore him if he starts sniffing around tonight."

"Promise. I have no interest—"

Joe grabs me around the shoulders with ninja-like reflexes as I trip on my dress and almost face plant on the stairs. He steadies me while I try to get my sandal untangled from the hem.

"You have a little pre-party before you headed this way?" he says, shaking his head.

"No, I'm not a big drinker. I just can't walk in long dresses for some reason. I'm not sure why I wear them. You know what I mean?"

"Yeah, I don't wear them much myself." He starts guiding me to the VIP area.

The bar's at the back of the hotel right off the beach. It's protected from the public boardwalk by a row of massive palm trees. The strings of white lights wrapped around their trunks make it hard for fans and paparazzi to get clear pictures of the celebrities as they enter the bar.

I see a bunch of heads poking through the trees as we walk to the entrance. They're holding their phones out and yelling for us to look their way. I don't know who they think I am. I can't imagine why they'd want a picture of me. It's horrifying—especially for my introverted brain. Joe doesn't seem to notice. I guess he deals with it a lot. The bouncer at the roped entrance nods at Joe as we walk through.

"All right," he says, still looking at his phone. His total indifference toward me is impressive. "You're in. My job's done here."

"Thanks for getting me in," I say, looking back at him as I walk away. "I'll see you around."

"I thought you promised that I wouldn't see you around," he says, pointing at me. "You're a distraction, remember?"

"Right. Right. Forget we ever met."

"I wish I could," he says, sighing, "but I have the feeling we'll be seeing each other again."

I watch him walk up the stairs to the VIP deck that's one level up from the main patio. He makes his way through the tables until he gets to the center. Joe's client is walking up to the most visible, high-profile table. Everyone on the patio's looking up—taking pictures of him. He looks down for a second and then does his best to ignore the people yelling at him from below.

I stand on tiptoe to get a better look. I've never seen him before. He might be an actor, but he's probably an athlete. He's huge—well over six feet with a massive, muscly body. His arms are particularly nice, busting out of the sleeves of his fitted white T-shirt. Really, everything's good—the arms, the chest, the shoulders. And his hair's falling down his neck in messy waves. I'm thinking about how I'd like to run my fingers through his curls when a shrill scream breaks me out of my trance.

"Sophie!" I look across the patio to see Savannah standing on her chair waving her arms over her head—like she's trying to guide a plane into its gate at the airport. When I wave, she rolls her eyes and plops down on her chair.

She's right underneath Famous Guy's table. I look up at him again. Joe's leaning down, saying something right into his ear. When Joe moves back, Famous Guy turns around and looks toward where I'm standing. He looks right at me. I pretend I don't see him.

As I start weaving through the tables on the lower deck, some guy grabs a handful of my dress and pulls me back toward him.

"Not so fast," he slurs. "I haven't seen you here before. How about we get to know each other a little better?"

I yank my dress out of his hand and slam my foot into his leg. I kick him so hard that his chair rams into the guy sitting next to him. Everyone at their table stops talking and glares at me—like I've done something wrong.

"Keep your hands to yourself, asshole." I point at the drunk guy and then point around to everyone at the table— daring them to challenge me. I don't have time for that kind of bullshit.

I turn back around and glance up at Famous Guy again. He's still looking at me—this time grinning from ear to ear. My first instinct is to flip him off, but instead, I feel my face forming a smile. I'm not sure what's happening right now. I hate celebrities. They're arrogant and boring and generally a waste of time, but there's something about this guy. I fight the urge to look up at him again, but I can feel him still staring at me.

"Everyone stop what you're doing!" Savannah's voice is too loud again and it's dripping with sarcasm. "The queen has finally arrived. And all eyes are on her as usual."

I give her my best "fuck you" smile and run around the table to hug Maisie who's beaming at me from underneath her bridal crown.

"Sorry I'm late, Mae," I whisper as she pulls me to her.

"You're always late, Soph," she says, kissing my cheek as she hands me a folding hand fan. "And you're *always* worth the wait."

I unfold the fan to see that it says, "I'm the Maid of Honor and the Number One Fan of the Bride."

"Nothing has ever been more accurate," I say, laughing as I fan myself. "I'm at your service, Madame Bride. Whatever you want to do tonight, I'll make it happen."

Chapter Four

SEB

"Seb Miller! Seb Miller!" My childhood friend Ricky screams at me as I walk toward the table. "Oh my God, can I have your autograph?"

As usual, my friends have chosen the most visible table at this stupid bar. They enjoy my fame way more than I do.

"Sit down, asshole," I laugh as I shove him on the shoulder.

Everyone on the lower deck is looking up and taking my picture. It's weird and annoying. The bar's designed to make the VIP level highly visible to the guests on the deck below. That always seems ironic to me since they do everything they can to hide the bar from people who aren't lucky enough to get in.

To get to the VIP entrance, you have to walk by a row of palm trees that block the bar from public view. People peer between the tree trunks at arriving celebrities. I always feel like they're looking at me through the bars of my cage at the zoo.

"Did you have to choose this table?" I sigh as I sit down. "And this bar? It's the worst."

"If by 'the worst' you mean the most amazing place on earth, then yes, we had to choose it," Ricky says without looking at me. He's still waving at the fans below.

Ricky's one of my three remaining friends. The other two, Paul and Stone, are smiling at me from the other side of the table. We've known each other since our grade school days back in Michigan. They still live in the little town where we grew up. They visit me every couple months to make sure I'm not letting the fame go to my head. Besides my parents and my little sister, they're the only people I trust anymore.

We had another guy in our group growing up, but I had to cut him loose. He asked me for autographed baseballs for his family and then sold them. He made about twenty grand. The crazy thing is that if he needed money, I would have given it to him in a second—no questions asked. I've known him since we were eight years old. When you get famous, you have to watch everyone.

"Quite a crowd in front," Stone says, handing me a beer from the iced bucket in front of him. "Anyone get an autograph?"

"Yeah." I take a long drink. "A little girl named Belle."

"Did you see any older girls in the crowd that might get more than an autograph from you tonight?" Ricky pulses his eyebrows and grins like the Cheshire Cat. I throw my bottle cap at him.

"Naw, nothing caught my eye." My mind flashes back to

the blonde in the white dress. She caught my eye. I hope Joe got her into the bar because I need to know a lot more about her.

"Nothing you even want to pass on to me?" Ricky loves coming to visit because he gets to bat cleanup for me. I'm never interested in the fangirls that flock around. Ricky, on the other hand, is very interested.

"I wouldn't even subject my worst enemy to a night with you."

"Well, no worries, easy picking here tonight." Ricky points past me to the table that's just over my shoulder, one level down. "Bachelorette party below, and not a loser in the bunch."

I shake my head. "Why are you the way you are?"

"Because God blessed me with all this greatness when I was born—"

"Can you leave him at home next time?" I turn to Paul and accept the fist bump he offers.

"You know I try every time, but somehow he always makes it on the plane," Paul says, looking over my shoulder. He nods. "What's up, Joe? Good to see you again."

"Hey, fellas. Glad you made it in okay." Joe leans down and whispers to me, "White dress just cleared the VIP entrance."

I nod and try to look subtly over my shoulder. I see her immediately. She's looking up at me. The minute she sees me looking, she looks down and takes off across the deck. Her long dress is blowing behind her as she power walks to her table. Some guy catches the tail of her dress as she passes his table. She almost falls backward as he tugs at it. He says something to her and all the guys at his table laugh.

I'm about to run down there and break his hand. My body tenses up until she whips the dress away from him and kicks him hard in the leg. She says something back to him and points at everyone around the table. They all stop talking and look down. Damn, she keeps getting more attractive.

She looks up at me and sees me grinning at her like a maniac. I try to control my face, but it's not possible. There's something about her that's made me lose any little bit of swagger I thought I had. I see a slight smile come to her lips before she looks down again. She starts walking in my direction. As she gets closer, I hear an ear-piercing voice below me.

"Everyone stop what you're doing!" The woman in the neon orange dress at the bachelorette table—who's been staring at me since I got here—is screaming. "The queen has finally arrived. And all eyes are on her, as usual."

Orange dress isn't wrong about that. My eyes haven't left the blonde once. She ignores orange dress and runs around the table to hug the woman wearing a crown. I'm guessing she's the bride-to-be.

"It's not my fault I'm late!" the blonde says as she collapses into a chair, fanning herself with one of those fold-up fans. "Security was holding everyone back so some guy could get in."

"What guy?" Orange dress looks up at me and winks. I look away. She's the kind of fangirl I hate.

"Do I know, Savannah?" The blonde lets out a long sigh. I can't help but stare at her chest as it rises and falls. I would do anything to get a better look. "You know I don't know who anyone is. That's your department."

"Was he an actor or singer?" Orange dress looks up at me again. "Or maybe even an athlete?"

The bride starts laughing. "Like she knows who an athlete is, Savannah. She hates sports."

"I don't hate sports," the blonde says, accepting a glass of champagne from the waiter who annoyingly also seems to be looking at her chest. "I just don't obsess about them like you do. And I don't care who the guy was. All I know is he made me late. It's his fault, not mine."

I smile to myself as I turn back around to the guys. I made her late. Damn, I'm going to have to find a way to make that up to her. I have so many ideas of how I can do just that.

Chapter Five

SOPHIE

"So, I heard Sam broke up with you?" Savannah tries to look concerned. I'm not sure why she even bothers.

"Damn, Van." Serena shoves her. She's the only one of our friends who can come close to controlling Savannah. "She just got here. Let her have a second."

"I broke up with him but you already know that." I down the rest of my champagne. I didn't want to drink tonight, but being around Savannah for more than a few minutes makes it necessary.

"Why'd you break up with him?" Maisie's future sister-in-law, Cate, pats my hand. "If you don't mind me asking."

"I don't. He cheated on me with his assistant." I take a long, deep breath. "Really original, huh?"

"That's why you need to stop dating boys," Taylor says as she pours me more champagne.

"I don't date boys. Sam's only a year younger than me."

"A year younger in age, but about a decade younger in maturity. He's still a bro. You know what I mean?"

"Tay, seriously, I haven't known what you've meant once in the eight years I've known you." I lean back in my chair, finally feeling relaxed. The champagne's already starting to kick in.

"I mean," she says, leaning forward, "that his mind's back in college. He's still in the learning stage. You need someone who will be an adult with you—and maybe even be able to teach you something."

"I can think of someone who'd like to be your teacher— for tonight anyway." Savannah looks over my head again—up to the VIP level. She's been doing that since I sat down. I tilt my head backward. Famous Guy's looking down, but he's not looking at Savannah. His eyes are fixed on me. I jerk my head up.

"Oh my God. Is he eavesdropping on us? That's the guy who made me late. Does anyone know who he is?"

Taylor opens her mouth, but Savannah slugs her. "Stop! No one tell her. Let's make her guess."

"I don't want to guess because I don't care who he is."

I hear him laugh above me. I'm about to tell him to mind his own business, but I don't even want to give him that much attention.

"He's been looking at you since you walked in." Savannah looks up at him again and then glares at me. Her mouth's pouty like it gets when anyone's receiving more attention than her.

"Aww, what's wrong, Savannah?" Maisie laughs. "Can't

you get him to look at you? Maybe you should wear a brighter dress next time."

"Is there a brighter dress than this somewhere in the world?" Serena pulls at Savannah's sleeve. "Seriously, I didn't know this color of orange existed."

Savannah pulls her sleeve away. "Not everyone can wear orange and look this good, Serena. And I'm married. I don't want guys to look at me anymore."

We all burst out laughing. "You've wanted guys to look at you—and only you—from the second you were born," I say, trying to catch my breath. "You were probably trying to hook up with the doctor right after you left the birth canal."

"Yeah, Van, did you have a onesie in this color when you were a baby?" Taylor pulls at her dress from the other side.

Serena tries to pour me another refill.

"No, babe," I say, putting my hand over the glass. "I have to work tomorrow. I can't be hungover."

"Who has to work on a Saturday?" Savannah says, pouring herself another glass of champagne.

"A lot of people, Savannah." I try to make my voice as condescending as possible. "Do you see all of the stores, restaurants, and gas stations that are open on the weekend? People work inside of them."

"Oh, don't get all power to the people on me. You don't work at a gas station," she says. "You own your own business. Could you not give yourself the day off?"

"I can't. I have the first meeting with a potential new client tomorrow—"

"That you can't talk about," Serena says.

"Nope. I've already signed the non-disclosure."

"Non-disclosure?" Cate says. "What kind of business do you own?"

"I'm a communications consultant—mainly crisis stuff. Companies call me when something goes wrong. I can never talk about it."

"No one wants to talk about it tonight." Savannah sighs loudly. "We're at a bachelorette party, not a business forum. And I think it's time we play a little game." She sweeps her hand in the air as our waiter sets a bottle of tequila right in the middle of our table.

"No!" I slam my back against the chair. "I am not playing Truth or Tequila tonight. Hell no!"

"Oh, really?" Savannah laughs. "Because I seem to remember a pact we made when we graduated that we'd play it five more times at each of our bachelorette parties."

"Maisie!" I look at her—my eyes pleading.

She holds my hand. "Soph, we did make a pact."

"We played it at my bachelorette, then at Tay's, then Serena's, and now at Maisie's." Savannah's folding her fingers down to count each one until only one finger's remaining up—her middle finger. She holds it up to me. "And if you can ever find a man to marry you, then we'll play it at yours."

"Do I even want to ask what Truth or Tequila is?" Cate looks justifiably worried.

"No, you don't," I say, burying my face in my hands. "Unfortunately, we've been playing it since our first week of college. It's the *Mean Girls* version of Truth or Dare."

"That's why Sophie always wins," Savannah says, screwing off the top of the tequila bottle. "Mean girl to the core."

"Please. You're the only mean girl at this table. I just haven't met a dare that I won't do—no matter how hard you try to come up with one."

"So, there are dares in the game?" Cate's eyes are racing around the table.

Maisie puts her hand on Cate's shoulder. "Basic rules: you choose between telling someone the truth or doing a shot of tequila. The twist is that these bitches," she says, pointing around the table, "get to choose who you tell the truth to and what the truth is. The goal is to make the truth so awful that you force your opponents to drink."

"That sounds horrible," Cate says. "Can they make something up that you have to tell someone?"

"Oh no. We don't have to make stuff up," Maisie says. "We tell each other way too much about how we feel about exes, friends, and family. This game capitalizes on that."

Cate laughs. "Well, none of you know that much about me, so I can probably win—"

"I know enough about you." Maisie sits back and peers over her sunglasses. "Like how you hate your sister's husband. How'd you like to call Sarah and tell her that?"

"You wouldn't—"

"Oh, I would," Maisie says, smiling. "It's part of the game. And I can use that truth every time it's your turn, so you either have to call her or drink."

Cate shakes her head and frowns. "When does the game end? Or does everyone just drink tequila all night?"

"You don't want to get drunk because when the group determines you're too drunk to have another shot, then you have to perform a dare that, of course, the group gets to choose. The game ends when someone completes a dare."

"If Sophie always wins, I guess she can hold more tequila than the rest of you."

Everyone collapses on the table laughing except for Cate and me.

Savannah lifts her head just enough to spit out, "Sophie's the biggest lightweight ever. She can't hold anything. It's why she doesn't want to play."

"I don't want to play because we're grown-ass women now, and the only reason you never get drunk is because you have absolutely no filter." I shove the table toward her. She looks up again. "The last time we played you told your mother-in-law that her breath smelled."

"Well, it does," she says, sitting back and crossing her arms.

"Yeah, and now the poor woman eats so many Altoids, her teeth are going to rot out by the time she's sixty."

"This game sounds horrible," Cate groans. "How do we make it end quickly?"

"Get Sophie drunk because she's the biggest lightweight," Serena says, "and then we challenge her to a dare that she always does. Game over."

"You get a little liquid courage, huh?" Cate says, nudging me.

"I get a little liquid stupid. Most liquor makes me silly. Tequila makes me crazy—absolutely no inhibitions left at all."

"It's so fun! I love tequila-drunk Sophie," Serena laughs.

"I will play this stupid game one more time." I point my

finger around the table. "This is the last time. I don't want it at my bachelorette. Agreed?"

"Well, none of us want to play it when we're fifty anyway." Savannah taps her fingers on the table as she flashes a devilish smile at me. "So, agreed. Now how about we start this round with you?"

"I'm sure you want me to call Sam, so pour me a shot right now." I reach toward the bottle. Savannah pulls it back.

"Don't you even want to know what I want you to tell him. It might not be that bad."

"Fine," I huff. "What?"

"I want you to call him and tell him," she says, leaning forward on the table, "that he never gave you an orgasm."

I cover my eyes and shake my head. "Why, why, why do I tell you people these things?"

"Wait," Serena says, pulling my hands off my face. "You dated him for six months. He never once gave you an orgasm. How is that possible?"

"Is his penis really small?" Cate reaches for my hand and pats it like a mother consoling her child.

I look at Maisie for help. She shoots me her concerned eyes, but she can't keep a smile from breaking out all over her face.

"His penis is fine," I say, looking up at the sky. "It's just— he wasn't very good with his hands."

"Or his mouth."

"Maisie!" I shove her. "You're supposed to be on my side here."

"Oh, honey, I am." She pats my shoulder. "No woman should have to deal with that."

"Maisie's right, Sophie," Cate says. "That's not negotiable. Nick is *very* good in that area."

"Uh! Cate!" Maisie glares at her. "I don't want to know that about my brother."

"Not to mention, now we can use that against you in this game." Taylor points at her from across the table.

"Oh, I've told him how good he is with his mouth," Cate says, savoring every word, "and I'm more than happy to tell him again."

"Oh my God, stop, please." Maisie throws her hands over her ears. "Can we please get on with the game?"

"Yeah, what's it going to be, Soph?" Savannah holds up the tequila bottle. "Are you calling Sam or not?"

"I'm not calling that jackhole for any reason, so you might as well attach a tequila drip to my arm for the night." I slam the shot that Savannah pushes across the table. "Ah, the taste of bad decisions and regret."

I turn to Maisie as Savannah moves onto her next victim. "Stop me before I get in too far. I have to at least look like I have a pulse for my meeting tomorrow."

Chapter Six

SEB

"Incoming!" Ricky points to the steps that separate the VIP level from the main deck.

The blonde in the white dress is trying to make her way up —trying very unsuccessfully. She cleared the first layer of security. They generally give women who look like her a free pass. Her main obstacles seem to be the stairs themselves. Every time she tries to take a step up, her long dress tangles with her feet. She tries to hold it up a little but keeps tripping on it.

Finally, she grabs it, yanks it up so it's barely covering her butt, and marches up the stairs. When she makes it to the top, she drops the dress back down, but not before every guy in the bar—including me—has his eyes glued to her. She looks over at our table, sighs, and starts walking toward us.

Ricky turns his chair around to face her and pats his lap. "Come here, little Mamacita. Tell Uncle Ricky what's wrong."

I kick his chair so hard that he tips over and ends up face-down on the deck. He turns his head to me.

"Mine," I growl as I point at him.

"Damn, Seb," he says as he pushes himself up. "Just tell me. You don't have to launch me into tomorrow."

She looks at Ricky and then back at me. I don't think she's registering what happened. I've been watching her table most of the night. They're playing some game, and she's losing badly. She's had way too much to drink, and it looks like the tequila's taken over her brain.

As she closes the distance between us, she gets tangled up in her dress again. She trips and falls forward. I leap up, sweep her into my arms, sit down, and place her on my leg in one fluid motion.

Her eyes are closed as she shakes her head a few times trying to figure out what just happened. She opens them up, squinting at me.

"Nice catch," she says, smiling as she tries to steady herself on my leg. I wrap my arm around her waist to help her out.

"Thanks. You might say I do that for a living."

She looks up at me—still squinting. "You catch people for a living?" I can tell by the blank expression on her face that she has no idea I'm a baseball player, much less a catcher.

"Pretty much."

She shifts around again. Her butt feels nice on my leg—too nice. She wiggles a little bit more. She's pretty much giving me a lap dance at this point. She needs to quit doing it before things get too active south of my belt.

"So is there something I can help you with tonight?" I say,

tightening my grip around her waist to stabilize her. "Or did you just come up here to say hi to me?"

She ignores my question as she looks around at the other guys, and then tilts her head up to look at Joe, who's standing a few feet behind me. She scrunches up her face and tries to focus on him.

"Is he a security guy?" She nods her head up at him and then looks back at me. "Are you someone?"

"I'm no one." I point to Ricky. "He's the important one. They're all here to protect him."

"Who is he?" She leans in toward my face and tries to whisper, but Ricky still hears her.

"I'm a Latin pop star—very popular in Miami." He winks at her and blows her a kiss.

"I don't believe you," she says as she drapes her arm comfortably around my neck. Her chest is inches from my face. I try to look away, but it's not possible.

"Smart woman," Paul says. "Don't believe a word Ricky says."

She points at Ricky and makes little circles with her finger. "You're lying and I think you're up to no good—"

"She's perceptive, too," Stone says.

She nods at Stone like they're in on this together. She looks back at Ricky. "Sing something."

Ricky starts singing—loudly and severely off-key. He reaches toward her as he tries to hit a high note. I swat his arms away.

She leans into my head until her forehead's resting above my ear. "He's not a very good singer," she says, annunciating each word. Her breath is going directly into my ear. It feels way too good.

I turn my head, so my mouth's up against her ear. "You've had too much to drink," I whisper.

She sits up suddenly, causing her butt to slip backward off my leg. I catch it with my hand and push her back up. I couldn't tell from underneath her dress, but now that I have a handful of it, I can tell her butt's incredibly round—just the way I like it.

She puts her finger in my face, oblivious to the fact that my hand's still on her ass. "That's why I'm here."

"Explain," I say, laughing as I slip my arm back around her waist.

"We're playing a game called Truth or Te-kia. Tuh-kee-uh."

"Tequila."

"Yes," she says, tapping my nose with her finger. "If you don't want to tell the truth, you have to drink."

"Well, from your current state, I'm guessing you've been lying all night."

"No, noooooo." She flings her legs over my other leg, trying to sit fully on my lap. My legs are spread too wide, so she falls between them. I close them quickly around her before she slams to the ground.

"Oopsies." She rests her head back on my leg as she looks up at me, smiling. She's hanging off my legs like a kid on a jungle gym.

"Yes, very much oopsies." I grab her under the arms and pull her back up onto my lap. "Are you okay?"

She ignores me again. "I haven't been lying. I just don't

want to tell the truth, so I had to drink—a lot. I'm not a very good drinker."

"I can see that, and I think you've had enough to drink for the night."

"Yes," she says, nodding, "that's why I have to do a dare to win the game."

"What's the dare?"

"I have to get you to kiss me." She puckers up and leans into me. I put my hand over her mouth and push it back.

"Not so fast," I say as her face melts into confusion. I'm sure I'm the only guy who's ever refused to kiss her. "I'm not that easy. I like to get to know someone before I kiss them."

"Mmmm," she says, wiggling her lips against my hand. I lift it to see a frown. "Just kiss me. It's easy. Just a smack and then we can be done."

"I'm not so sure I want to be done," I say, tapping my fingers on my chin. "Tell me something about yourself first. Let's start with your name."

She lets out a dramatic sigh. "Sophie. I mean Sophia."

"Do you not know what your name is?"

She leans in closer to my face and whispers again. "My friends call me Sophie, but I like to be called Sophia in business."

"Okay, Sophie," I whisper back to her.

"We're not friends."

"We don't work together either."

She tilts her head back and laughs silently—like I've said something funny.

"You're funny," she says, laying her head on my shoulder. "Tell me a joke."

"I don't really tell jokes." The top of her head's pressed against my face. Her hair smells like oranges. "I'll tell you a secret though."

She lifts her head and looks at me suspiciously. "What secret?"

"I've been eavesdropping all night on your game. I know your friends dared you to kiss me so you wouldn't have to call your ex-boyfriend."

"Sam," she says, spitting his name like she's trying to get poison out of her mouth.

"Is that his name?"

"That was his name."

"Was? Is he dead now?"

"He's dead to me!" She smiles broadly again as she closes her eyes and scrunches up her nose. She lets out a few chuckles. She's very pleased with her joke.

Her eyes pop open. "Wait, is your name Sam?" She's so serious suddenly. Even if my name were Sam, I think I'd lie to her.

"It's Seb."

"Sep?"

"Seb."

"Sep-p-p-p." She lets it drain out of her mouth slowly, popping every "p" with her perfect lips. "Sep is a weird name."

"Sep is a weird name. It's not my name, but it's definitely weird."

"You said your name was Sep." She taps me on the nose again.

"I said my name was Seb. It's short for Sebastian."

"Oh!" She sits up straight. "My neighbors had a cat named Sebastian. We called him Sebbie. Can I call you that?"

"You definitely cannot call me that."

She sighs again and lays her head back on my shoulder. "I didn't want to call Sam, so I had to drink tuh-keeee-luh. I don't like it very much."

"I don't think tequila likes you very much either." I take a whiff of her hair again. It smells so good. "Why didn't you want to call him?"

"He's awful," she says into my chest. "He cheated on me."

"He is awful. And it sounds like he's stupid, too."

"He is stupid." She sits up again and leans in until her eyes are inches from mine. "Your eyes are blue."

"Yep—"

"And they're ripply. They look like ocean waves."

"I don't think my eyes are ripply," I say, putting my forehead against hers. "I think your vision is a little blurry right now."

"I like looking at your eyes," she says as she yawns right into my face. She tries to cover it with her hand but ends up smacking the side of my head.

"Okay, I think it's time to get you home. You're done for the night." I look down at her table of friends and motion the one with the crown to the stairs. "Joe, let her up."

"I have to kiss you first or I won't win the game," Sophie says as her head bobs to her chest.

"Not going to happen," I say, lifting her chin. "I only kiss sober women."

"I'm drunk," she says. She's staring right into my eyes again. I like looking at her eyes, too. They're the lightest brown I've ever seen, accentuated by sparkling flecks of green.

"Yes, you are drunk, and you need to go to sleep."

"Okay." She puts her head back down on my shoulder and lets out a sigh. By the time her friend makes it up to us, she's almost fallen asleep on my chest.

"Sophie." Her friend shakes her shoulder. "Wake up. It's time to go home."

Sophie stirs a little bit and looks up. "Maisie!"

"Hey, Soph. It's time to call it a night," Maisie laughs as she reaches for Sophie's hands and pulls her off my lap. Sophie falls into her.

"Why don't I help you get her to the car?" I say, grabbing Sophie's shoulders to steady her. She leans back against me.

Joe steps between us. "Seb, you can't leave with a drunk girl. Too many cameras here."

"We have a suite upstairs," Maisie says, pointing to her bride crown. "My bachelorette party. I think I can get her up to the room myself."

"Joe, get her to the elevators." I pass Sophie off to him. "I'll meet you there."

"Seb," Joe says, raising his eyebrows.

"Just do it. It'll be fine. I want to make sure they get up there safely."

I sit back down to give the crowd time to put their phones away. I wait a few minutes before I take a roundabout way to the elevators—the rest of Joe's security team following behind me. The elevators are hidden behind a row of palms. As I duck behind them, I see Joe holding a door open.

"Sep!" Sophie dives into my open arms as I walk in.

"Hi, Soph." I wrap my arms around her. "You doing okay?"

"I don't feel good, Sep."

"I know. You're going to feel a lot worse tomorrow."

She groans against my chest as her legs buckle. I sweep her into my arms as the elevator door opens.

"Wait." Joe holds his hand up to block me from walking out. He turns to Maisie. "What room are you in?"

"602."

"Go unlock it and wait for us there with the door open." Maisie looks from him to me.

"We'll be down in a second," I say, nodding my head toward Joe. "He's just doing his job. We don't want anyone to get a picture of this—for her sake, too. Believe me."

Joe looks up and down the hallway a few more times and then motions me toward the room. Maisie's waiting for us at the door.

"Here," she says, pointing at one of the attached bedrooms off the suite. "Let's put her in this bedroom. It has its own bathroom. She's probably going to need it tonight."

Maisie runs ahead of me and fluffs the pillows on the bed.

"You're cute," Sophie says as I place her on the bed.

"Yeah, you're cute, too." I brush her hair off her face as she smiles up at me.

"But you don't want to kiss me."

I pull the covers up to her chin. "I want to—believe me."

"But I'm drunk."

"Yes, you are," I whisper, "and you need to go to sleep."

"I'll go to sleep if you kiss me." She tries to wink at me but just scrunches up her face instead. It's so cute.

I shake my head. "Do you promise?"

"Yes," she whispers, tilting her head and smiling.

I take her face gently into my hands. Her eyes close as I lean down and touch her lips. "Go to sleep now, Sophie."

She turns and buries her face in the pillows. "I won, Sep," she mumbles.

"Yeah, you did," I say as I pull the blankets up a little higher.

When I turn around, Maisie's standing by the door.

"Are you going to make sure she doesn't die tonight?" I frown as she takes a few more steps into the room and closes the door.

"That's been my job since we were like ten," she says, walking over to the bed. She tilts Sophie's head up so her nose and mouth are free of the pillows. Sophie lets out a deep breath.

"You suck at your job. You're lucky I'm the one you dared her to kiss. Someone else might have taken advantage of this situation. Do you know how dangerous this is?"

"You know, from your reputation," she says, moving the trash can to the side of the bed, "I'd think you'd be the one I'd have to worry about—"

"Don't believe everything you read," I growl as I head toward the door.

"Her last name is Banks if you ever want to call her. Sophia Banks."

I whip around. "You let her get in this condition and now you're trying to pimp her out?"

"I'm not trying to pimp her out."

"Could have fooled me."

41

"Despite what I've read about you and what I'm seeing at this very second," she says, "you seem very sweet, and I can tell you like her. Sophie needs somebody sweet after her last boyfriend."

"I'm not that sweet." I turn back toward the door. "Believe me."

She follows me out into the suite's sitting area. The rest of the group have made it back and are draped over the furniture.

"Oh my God!" The loud one in the orange dress jumps up from the couch. "Seb Miller's in my suite!"

She pulls out her phone. Joe swipes it away from her and points at the other women who slowly drop their phones. "No pictures," he barks.

"One group picture is fine." I turn to Maisie. "If you want one."

"That would be nice. Thank you." She smiles at me. I smile back. She seems okay.

"Take it so it doesn't look like I'm in a hotel room with five women," I say, turning to Joe.

"What? Am I new to this job?" He laughs. "Up against that blank wall."

Orange dress pushes another woman out of the way to get next to me and then snakes her arm around my waist, letting her hand sink to my butt. "Sophie's going to be so jealous she missed this picture!"

"I doubt that very much." I step away from her quickly after Joe takes the picture.

She follows me. "Wait, did you close the deal? Did you kiss her? Or did you do even more than that?"

I glare at her. Maisie gets between us and starts pushing

me toward the door. "No, he didn't kiss her. He was a perfect gentleman. He just helped me get her up to the room."

As I step into the hallway, I turn back around. "What'd you say her last name was again?"

"Banks," Maisie says. "Google Sophia Banks. She has a consulting firm. You can call her on her business number."

"Or you could just give me her cell number," I say, smiling as I hold up my phone.

"If you want that, you're going to have to earn it yourself." She smiles as she backs into the room. "I don't pimp out my best friend, remember?"

"Right," I say, laughing.

Joe closes in on me. "We've got to go, man. Media in the building."

I look back to the suite's door. As Maisie disappears behind it, I hear her say, "Goodnight, Sep."

———

Chapter Seven

SOPHIE

"I hate you so much." My head's resting on my steering wheel as I look down at the phone on my lap. Maisie's head—still resting comfortably on a pillow—fills the screen.

"Soph," she whispers. I can't see her mouth. I only see half of one of her eyes peeking through her hair, "I'm hungover, too."

"Yeah, but you get to sweat out the tequila by the hotel pool today. I have to act like a functioning human."

I look in the rearview mirror. Somehow, I managed to take a shower this morning, but it didn't help at all. I'm so pale. I look like I've been dead for about two weeks.

"What time's your meeting?" She moves the hair off her face. It falls back down. Now, I can't even see half an eye. I'm just staring at her hair.

"In about five minutes," I say, closing my eyes. It's the only way my head feels tolerable. "That gives you about two minutes to tell me what I did last night. Who was the guy I

44

tried to seduce? It was like Seth or Sutton—something with an "s." The only things I remember about him are his eyes. They were so blue. I can still see them."

"His name's Seb."

"What kind of name is Seb?"

"Soph, how do you not know who he is? He's the catcher—"

My phone's alarm goes off. We both groan. I slap at the screen until I finally hit the right spot to turn it off. "That was aggressively loud. I've got to go. You can tell me more about him tonight. You didn't give him my number, did you?"

"Not technically—"

"Mae, I've told you to stop doing that." I look in the mirror once more. Still no good. "I'll be back to the hotel by five. I'm not drinking tonight. Nothing. Not even a glass of wine. Just comfort food and movies, please."

"Yeah, I already told everyone tonight's canceled. I can't take another night of Savannah. She's getting worse, right?"

"Somehow, she is. I don't even know how that's possible. I'll call you later."

"Okay," she yawns. "You can do this, Sophie."

"Sophia Banks."

Gary Randall peers at me from behind his enormous desk. It stretches almost the entire length of the small office and it's unusually tall. He stands up and extends his hand. At least I think he's standing. His waist barely clears the top of the desk.

"It's nice to meet you, Mr. Randall." I walk around the

desk and shake his hand. I'm towering over him. I'm about five-nine-ish with my heels, and at least a head taller than him. He has to crane his neck to look me in the eyes. The snarky look on his face, makes me wish I'd worn flats.

He motions toward a chair. I drop into it to try to ease his Napoleon complex, but also because the walk from the parking garage has left me exhausted and dehydrated. I'd do anything for a glass of water.

"Roman Garcia raves about what you did for his company." Gary finally sits down. He must be sitting on a really high chair because somehow he's looking down at me.

"He's very kind." I manage to get out.

"Well, I don't know about that." He lets out a sharp laugh. It feels like someone stabbed my head with a spear. "He's kind of an asshole. He's gay as Tinkerbell but you can't cross him. He's part of that Cuban business Mafia. You know—"

"Wow," I say, putting my hand up to stop him. "Somehow, you managed to be homophobic and racist in that one statement."

"Excuse me!" He slaps his hands down hard on the desk. My head's pounding. "Who do you think you're talking to?"

I close my eyes as a bit of tequila manages to regurgitate into my mouth. I've already thrown up twice this morning. You'd think it would all be gone by now.

"Mr. Randall," I say, grabbing the sides of the chair to try to get control of my body again. "I didn't mean to offend you, as I'm sure you didn't mean to offend Mr. Garcia, but you hired me to help you with your organization's faltering reputation. Although you said your main concern is a potential sexual discrimination suit, we should start being careful—

organization-wide—about any kind of discriminatory behavior."

I smile at him. Just that small movement makes my head feel like it's about to explode.

He doesn't smile back. "I think you misunderstood what I said. It wasn't meant as an insult. I have gay friends and Cuban friends. Roman's both, and I consider him a good friend."

"It doesn't matter if you have friends—"

"Sorry I'm late, Dad." I turn around to see Gentry Randall sauntering into the office. He's a little taller than his dad, but he has the same aggressively receding hairline. He has on madras-plaid shorts, a white T-shirt with an enormous Balenciaga logo on the chest, and flip-flops. He stops dead in his tracks when I stand up.

"Well, hello, Sophia Banks," he says, slowly looking down the length of my body. "Dad didn't tell me you were going to look like this. Nice to have some eye candy in this place finally."

"Good Lord." I fall back into my chair, ignoring his outstretched hand. "Gentry, that's completely inappropriate to say in a business setting—really, in any setting."

He has the confused look on his face that every entitled man has when you challenge him.

"What?" He laughs as he falls into a chair beside me.

"Miz-z-z-z Banks," Gary says, drawing out the Ms. title like it's an insult, "I hired you to root out a problem that we have within our clubhouse, not to put a microscope on *my* family."

"No," I say, turning toward him. "You hired me to improve

your team's image. That involves correcting problems within the entire organization."

He leans forward on his elbows. "It involves what I say it involves."

I take a deep breath. It makes me feel like I'm going to throw up again. "Mr. Randall, we agreed that today's meeting was to determine if we're on the same page. If we're not, I'm happy to show myself out."

In fact, I'm more than happy to do that. There's nothing I want more than to be curled up in bed again.

"Your reputation is that you're the best in the business," he says, glaring at me. "Maybe we can start again, and please call me Gary."

Gary turns to Gentry. "Apologize to Ms. Banks."

Gentry looks like his dog just died. "I'm sorry," he says, still looking at his dad. "I just meant, uh, that you wear your clothes well."

Gary's head flips back to me to see if I'm going to let that one slide. I'm not.

"Okay, Gentry," I say, patting the arm of his chair. "Here's a trick I use with some of my other clients. WSM—white straight male."

"Hey, that's me!" Gentry points to himself proudly.

"Yes, very good," I say, trying to keep my voice from being too condescending. "So this should be easy for you. The trick is: before you say something to anyone, think to yourself, 'Would I say this to a WSM—white straight male?' If you wouldn't, then you shouldn't say it to the person in front of you either. For instance, if I had been a white straight male, would you have referred to me as 'eye candy' or told me that I wear my clothes well? I can see by the look on your face that you wouldn't have, so now you know you shouldn't have said it to me either."

He looks confused. I turn back to Gary. He's still scowling at me.

"Would you like to get started or should I show myself out?" I'm hoping he'll tell me to leave.

He seethes for a good minute before he finally says, "Roman said you spoke your mind, but I don't think I expected all of this."

"It can be a lot," I say, nodding, "but it's the quickest way to accomplish our goals."

"Hmm." He's not convinced, and from the look on his face, I think he'd like to slap me. "Why don't we test each other out for a few days and see how we feel after that? My attorney said you signed the non-disclosure agreement."

"I did." I settle back in my chair. The adrenaline that's now surging through my body is making me feel a little better.

"Then let's get started. The short version of the story is that our PR department banned Liza Murray from the team's clubhouse for a few days. She started making a fuss all over town that we did it because she was the only female reporter covering the team."

"Was that the reason?"

"I can't get a straight answer as to why it happened. My PR guy, Ken, says he did it because she left the newspaper and started a blog. He said her blog wasn't an accredited media source."

"But *she's* an accredited media member," I say. "She's been working in this market for five-plus years."

"As I said, I didn't get a good answer." He stops to take a long swig of his Diet Coke. "Her feeling is that one of the players asked that she be banned, but she won't say who she suspects."

"You've talked to her?" I look up from my notes.

"Yes, Gentry and I had a meeting with her. We agreed to reinstate her credentials if she'd stop talking about it."

"Are you paying her off?" Gary's eyes sink back into slits. "Gary, I have to know everything if I'm going to do my job effectively. I have a non-disclosure. Legally, I can't tell anyone anything you say, and I wouldn't anyway."

"We're not paying her off," he says, pausing for a second to consider his next words carefully, "but we think one of our players might be."

"For what reason? To keep her quiet about the clubhouse banning?"

"No, we think it's more than that—"

"We think she might have been fucking one of our players and he's paying her to keep quiet about it," Gentry says. "And I would say it just like that to a white straight male."

"Okay," I say, looking between them. "Which player?"

"We're not sure." Gary walks around his desk and motions toward the door, indicating that our meeting's coming to an end. "We're hoping you can figure it out. I've about reached my limit on the bad press we're receiving because of this. I don't want you to ask the players about it directly. Just get to know them and see if anything seems off to you. You might as well start now. They're taking BP on the field. Gentry can take you down there and introduce you around."

Gentry holds the elevator door open when we reach the field level. "I'd do this for a WSM, too," he says, winking at me.

"Okay, Gentry." My voice reflects the nausea that rockets back through my body as we step out of the air conditioning into the hellish humidity. "You don't have to vocalize it every time. Maybe just think it to yourself, but good job."

"Again, I'm sorry if I offended you," he says, motioning me to go ahead of him up the stairs to the field. "That's the absolute last thing I would want to do to you."

He makes that last part sound a little lewd. I want to punch him. He doesn't look like he's ever been in a fight in his life. I think I could at least knock him to the ground. He's making me really want to try.

"Well, let's just go by baseball rules." I sidestep him as he tries to put his hand in the small of my back. "You have two strikes. Try not to get that third."

"You know," he says, "some of the best home runs in history have been hit when the player had two strikes— speaking metaphorically, of course."

"Of course," I say, narrowing my eyes as I look at him. If I wasn't so close to throwing up again, I'd say more but as it is, I'm using all of my energy to control the bile that's trying to exit my body. As I step onto the field, the midday sun attacks me. I start sweating immediately. The sweat smells like tequila.

"Hey, are you Sophia?" A man—trying to type on a laptop while he walks—makes his way over to us. He's wearing khakis and a T-shirt that look like he pulled them out from the bottom of the hamper this morning.

"I'm Ken Burris," he says, looking at me with a weird combination of curiosity and suspicion. "I'm the VP of PR for the team. Gary told me you were coming in, although he never explained why."

"Hi," I say, extending my hand. He looks at it for a second before he shakes it. "I assure you I'm not here for your job if that's what you're thinking. No offense but I can't think of too many jobs I would want less."

He grunts but starts to smile a little bit. "Well, Gary said you were smart. Why are you here?"

"Just some corporate image stuff. No need to get territorial. I'll stay out of your way and be out of here as soon as possible."

"Hey, Dane! Dane!" Gentry's screaming at one of the players like he's an eight-year-old fan. "Dane, this is Sophia Banks. She's going to be working with the team."

Ken whispers, "If you can take Gentry off my hands for a few weeks, I might even like you before this is all over."

"Don't get too crazy," I whisper back.

"Dane!" Gentry's still yelling.

The guy he's yelling at turns around. "Quit yelling, man. I hear you." He nods his head at me and waves. "I'm Dane."

"Hey." I manage to wave back.

Gentry keeps yelling my name and pointing at me. Some of the players are smiling but most of them look annoyed. The player behind the plate jumps up and charges toward us.

Gentry takes a quick step back but still manages to say, "Seb! This is Sophia Banks."

The player walks right in front of me and pulls his catcher's mask up. I'm suddenly staring at the blue eyes I've been thinking about all morning.

"Sophie?" he says as a small smile starts to form at the corners of his mouth.

Chapter Eight

SEB

"Could you try to put a little something on it this time?" I growl out to the pitching coach who's been lobbing balls to me behind the plate.

I'm working on my throw to second. He's been tossing balls in here like he's pitching a softball game at a company picnic. In fairness to him, I've almost taken his head off a couple of times with my throw. At this point, I think he's just trying to get the ball over the plate and then get the hell out of my way.

My adrenaline's surging today. I've been thinking about Sophie non-stop since I tucked her into bed and kissed her last night. When I got back to my house, I immediately Googled her. I stared at her phone number for about thirty minutes before I got up the nerve to call her. I knew she'd still be passed out at the hotel, but I thought I'd leave a message. The minute I heard her greeting on the voicemail, I panicked and hung up like a thirteen-year-old boy with a crush.

I talked myself out of calling again. I'm not even sure what I'd say, "Hey, this is Seb Miller. You called me Sep all night while you were basically giving me a lap dance and then you fell asleep on my chest. When I tucked you in and kissed you, my body felt like it was going to explode. I'm sure you don't even remember me, but do you want to go out sometime?"

"Dane! Dane!" I hear Gentry's voice behind me. He's the owner's son and the most annoying fan out there. The only difference between him and other fans is that unfortunately, he has a lot more access to us. I swear I think some owners buy sports teams just so their kids can hang out with professional athletes.

Gentry's always down on the field bugging us. The players asked the GM several times not to let him on the field, but he keeps showing up. I guess the son of the guy who pays our salaries gets to do what he wants.

I try to ignore him, but his voice annoys the crap out of me. What's he saying? Something about banks. Wait, did he just say Sophia Banks?

I stand up as another ball crosses the plate. It hits me on the chest protector but doesn't even faze me. I spin around to see Sophie standing next to Gentry. For a second, I think I might be hallucinating. I walk quickly toward them.

"Sophie?" I say, raising my mask to get a better look.

She looks surprised—maybe even pleased—for a second, but then a look of panic spreads over her face.

"Wait," Gentry says, looking back to her. "Do you two know each other?"

"No!" Sophie glances at Gentry and then back to me. "I don't think we've ever met."

I can tell she recognizes me, but I decide to play along.

"No, I don't know her," I say, looking at Gentry. "Should I?"

"Because if you know each other, Sophia can't work here—"

"Are you deaf? I said I didn't know her." I take off my mask and rub the sweat off my face with my arm.

Sophie closes her eyes as a bead of sweat rolls down her forehead. She needs me to wipe the sweat off her face, too. In fact, her entire body's sweating and it looks like she's shaking a little. I'm guessing that's a hangover talking.

"But you called her Sophie," Gentry says.

"You've been behind me for a good five minutes screaming her name." I take a giant step so I'm inches from him. He backs up. "I don't know her. Who is she?"

"Oh, okay," Gentry says. "Yeah, so she's a new PR consultant. She's going to be hanging out with us for a while. Let me know if you ever need her to do anything."

I still have the overwhelming urge to take care of her that I had last night. I'm not sure what it is about her, but I pretty much want to protect her from everything and everyone. She closes her eyes again and sways a little too much, like she's about to pass out. I need to get her out of the heat.

"Yeah, actually, I could use her help right now with—uh, answering some fan mail."

"Oh," she says, squinting at me, "that's not really what I do—"

"Sophia!" Gentry yells. "Seb's our franchise player. If he

wants you to answer fan mail, then you should do it. It might be a good way for you to get to know him anyway. I could help, too."

I hold up my hand. "No, I don't need two people. Sophie, I mean Sophia, will be fine."

She's looking between us like we're crazy. "Yeah, I think I'm going to pass."

I lock my eyes with hers. "I mean if you don't want to sit in my *air-conditioned* office for a few hours. My quiet, cool office—"

"You know," she says as her eyes focus a little bit more, "reading your fan mail probably would help me get to know you a little better."

"Yeah, I thought so." I motion her toward the dugout.

"See you later, Seb!" Gentry yells at me as we walk away. "I'll be out here if you need me."

Sophie clings to the handrail as we walk down the three steps into the dugout. My arms are ready to catch her if she passes out.

"You have a rough night last night?" I say as I lead her to the tunnel that goes to the clubhouse.

"No," she whispers. "Just a little tired."

"Really? You seem like you're pretty hungover."

She tries to turn around to look at me but trips and falls into the wall. I grab her arm to steady her. "Or are you still drunk?" I say, laughing.

She spreads out on the concrete wall like she's waiting for someone to search her. "Oh my God," she groans, "this wall is so cold. It feels like heaven."

I grab her shoulder and point her down the tunnel again.

"Let's get moving before someone sees you trying to hump the wall."

"That wall is my friend, Seb."

"Well, at least you're calling me by the right name today."

I lead her down the hallway that goes behind the clubhouse. The team gave me a private office back here as part of my new contract. I wouldn't normally ask for that kind of special treatment, but I'm an introvert. I function better if I have a place to decompress alone. As we walk into my office, she drops her head back and stands right under the air-conditioning vent. Her hair's blowing behind her like she's doing a photoshoot.

"Oh my God." She arches her back farther. "This is amazing."

"Don't tilt back too far," I say, sliding my hand under her shoulders. "You might pass out. Here sit down on the bed."

She jolts upright. She looks at the bed and then back at me. I guess she didn't see it when she came in.

"Look, I don't know what you think is going to happen here," she says, pointing at the bed, "but that's not part of my job."

I take a few steps away from the bed—holding my hands in the air. "The only thing that's going to happen here is you taking a nap—by yourself."

"What? I thought I was supposed to answer your fan mail."

"My mom answers my fan mail."

"Aww, that's sweet." She smiles and then frowns again when I take a step toward her. I reach into the compartment below the bed and take out an extra blanket.

"There's water in here," I say, opening the refrigerator. "I suggest you drink a lot of it. There's Advil in my gym bag over there. I'll wake you up in like an hour or so."

She frowns. "How do I know you're not going to come in here while I'm sleeping?"

"Well, first, you look like hell, so don't flatter yourself." I smile at her as I back up toward the door. "And second, the door locks from the inside. These are my keys."

As I throw them to her, she covers her head like I lobbed a grenade at her. The keys hit her on the shoulder.

"Ow," she says, opening her eyes.

"I'm sorry." I grab the keys and toss them on the table next to my wallet and phone. "We're definitely going to have to work on your reflexes."

She looks from the table up to me. "You're going to leave that stuff in here with me?"

"I don't peg you as a felon, but if you are, my car's the black Range Rover. Drive it with care. I love it more than I love most people."

She looks up at me again, squinting her eyes. I shake my head as I take her arm and pull her reluctant body over to the bed. I push her shoulders down until she's sitting.

"You have control issues don't you?" she says, squinting her eyes.

"No."

"And self-awareness issues." She nods as she kicks off her shoes and crawls under the blankets.

"I thought Gentry said you were in PR, not psychology."

She lets out an appreciative moan as her head sinks back into the pillows. It takes every bit of discipline in my body not to crawl in with her. She's unbelievably attractive to me—the perfect combination of sweet and just smoldering hot.

"I can do both," she says, smiling as she pulls the blankets up to her chin. "Whatever you need."

Whatever I need? Fuck. I think I'm going to need a lot, but this isn't the time for that discussion. I can tell I'm going to have to take baby steps with her.

"Would you like me to tuck you in again or can you do it yourself this time?"

She squints at me again. I don't think she remembers much about last night. She has her eyes fixed on me as I back up toward the door. She looks like she's ready to bolt if I make any wrong moves. I stand out of the way, so she can see me turn the lock.

"Locks from the inside. See? You can check it when I leave." I turn off the lights as I close the door. "Go to sleep now, Sophie."

Chapter Nine

SOPHIE

"Sophie, wake up. Sophie."

When I open my eyes, Seb's kneeling by the bed, shaking me. It takes me a second to remember where I am, but when I do, I push him so hard that he loses his balance and ends up sprawled out on the floor. He scoots away from me until his back's up against the opposite wall.

"Good Lord, Sophie." He laughs, throwing his hands in the air. "You're stronger than you look. I come in peace. I was trying to wake you up. That's all."

"I thought you said I had the only keys to the room." I jump up and skirt around the edge of the room as I head for the door.

"I didn't say that. I said you have *my* keys." He points to the keys that are still where he left them on the table. "Security has an extra set—in case I lock myself out. I've been knocking on the door for like ten minutes. I thought you died."

He hangs his head, like a puppy that's been scolded.

"I'm sorry," I say, shaking my head. "I didn't mean to accuse you of anything."

"Yes, you did. It's okay, though. I have trust issues, too."

I frown at him. I don't like that he's figured me out so quickly. "How long have I been asleep?"

"Going on two hours. Do you feel any better?"

I take a quick mental scan of my body. "You know, I do. At least the headache's gone."

"Good." His eyes light up when he smiles again. I don't remember much about last night, but I was right about his eyes. They're intoxicating. "You can sleep some more if you want."

"No, I've got to find the Randalls." I look around the room for my shoes. "They're going to wonder where I am."

"You're fine. We don't have a game today. They've already left." He pulls himself onto a chair. He's rubbing his elbow. "I told them you were in my office going through a huge stack of fan mail."

"Thanks for covering for me." He's still rubbing his elbow. "Did I hurt your elbow? Are you going to have to go on the injured list or whatever?"

He grins at me. "Disabled list. And settle down. You're not that strong but I'm impressed. I'll think twice about touching you again."

"I'm sorry. I'm not usually this much of a train wreck. Last night was just—"

"Oh, I know what last night was." He's laughing now—like he knows way too much.

"I don't remember most of it."

"Shocking." He's still grinning at me. It's making me uncomfortable.

"I don't drink too often."

"Also shocking."

"And when I do, I get stupid. I hope I didn't say anything to offend you."

"Naw, you're good. You didn't say anything embarrassing."

"That would certainly be a first," I say, shaking my head. "Come on. Tell me what I said. I can take it."

"Well, let's see." He tilts his chair back and looks at the ceiling. "Um, you called me Sep all night instead of Seb. You told me your neighbors had a cat named Sebastian that you called Sebbie. You wanted to call me that. And you wanted me to kiss you so you could win a game called Truth or Tequila. Oh, and you said you liked looking at my eyes."

"Wow, wow, wow," I murmur as I cover my face. I peek out through my fingers. "I thought you said I didn't say anything embarrassing."

"It wasn't embarrassing. It was cute." He puts his chair back down and stares at me. I can tell he's trying to decide whether he should say this next part. I wish he wouldn't. "You also told me your boyfriend cheated on you, and I just want to say, I think he's the biggest idiot ever created."

"Gah," I groan, "way too much information. I also over-share when I'm drunk."

He holds up his hand when he sees the concern on my face. "That's the only secret you told me. I swear."

"You said something earlier about tucking me into bed—"

"Nothing happened. Your friend Maisie was there the

entire time. I made sure you got back to your room safely and then left. That's it. You don't remember any of that? I'm not even sure how you recognized me today."

"The eyes," I say, looking down. "I remember bits and pieces."

"I'm surprised you even approached me last night if you knew you were coming here today. Or were you too drunk to recognize me?"

"Oh God, I had no idea who you were, but honestly, I wouldn't have known if I was sober. No offense."

"None taken. It's kind of refreshing." He smiles as he looks at his phone. "It's kind of early for dinner, but you should probably get some food in your stomach. You want to grab something to eat with me?"

"Oh, Seb, thank you. That's nice, but I can't hang out with you. Despite what you've seen from me the past twenty-ish hours, I'm usually very professional including keeping my personal life separate from my work."

He nods. "How long will you be working here?"

"I don't know. My contracts usually go a month or so."

"Okay, then I would like to take you to dinner, but I don't want your answer for about a month."

"Seb—"

"No." He holds up his hands again. "I'm giving you a month to think about your answer. I don't want it before then."

"I'm going to say no right now. I don't date my clients even after the job's done."

His face hardens. "I'm not your client. The Randalls are. And speaking of them, watch your back."

"What does that mean?"

"It means they're rich, entitled assholes who think they can do anything they want." The muscles in his beautiful arms tense up. "Don't be alone with them, especially Gentry. Okay?"

"Okay. I think I should go."

"Sophie," he says, grabbing my hand as I walk around him to the door. He lets it go when I try to jerk it away. "I'm sorry. Just instinct. Thank you for not punching me this time. It's just —you seem really sweet. I like talking to you. Can we do a reset here? Maybe talk a little bit some time."

"Part of my assignment is to get to know the team, so yeah, of course, we can talk. It just can't be flirty—"

"I won't flirt with you," he says, smiling again as he opens the door for me. "But I can't control how you act toward me. I'm charming as hell. I'll understand if you need to flirt with me."

I try not to smile but end up laughing. "I think I'll be fine."

He steps in front of me. "Uh, can I get your cell number? You know for professional reasons."

"No," I say, laughing again. "You cannot."

"Put my number in your phone? Just in case you need me." He looks down. "I mean, you might need baseball tips or something."

"Baseball tips?"

He starts shifting back and forth. "Yeah, like if you ever have to know how to throw someone out at second or something. I'm your guy."

"You know I was in a situation the other day where I needed to do that. If I just would have had your number."

He points at my phone. "For next time. Start typing."

After I save his number in my phone, I shake my head and walk away, still smiling. I can feel his eyes watching me. It sends a warm feeling all the way through my body. I close my eyes as I try desperately not to turn around and look at him one more time.

Chapter Ten

SEB

"You need to keep your eyes on that one," I hear Joe say behind me as I watch Sophie walk away. She looks over her shoulder and smiles at me before she turns the corner. It's a flirty smile.

"Oh, I'll gladly keep my eyes on her." I turn around smiling, but Joe's got the snarl on his face that he only gets when someone's trying to get too close to me.

"Did you have sex with her?" He nods his head toward my office. "You've been in there for a while."

"No! What the hell, Joe?" I'm not smiling anymore. "You know me better than that."

"She's the girl from last night—"

"She's the *woman* from last night, but yeah, I know who she is. Her name's Sophie." I walk back into the office. Joe follows me.

"Don't you think it's a little suspicious that she happened to be there last night and then she shows up here today?"

I shake my head. "I think it's a coincidence—a nice one."

He looks at me—his eyebrows narrowing. "My pops always told me that coincidence was an excuse used by liars."

"Well, obviously your dad was as suspicious as you are," I growl. "She's not up to anything. She's not like that. She's sweet."

"They're always sweet until they're not," he says, sitting down at the table. "Do you know why she's here?"

"Yeah," I say slowly. I don't think I like where this is headed. "Gentry said she's here to do some kind of PR work."

"She's here to find out who's responsible for getting Liza Murray kicked out of the clubhouse. Gary told me."

"Huh," I say as I zip up my gym bag and throw it over my shoulder. "You think I should tell her it was me?"

"No! Are you crazy?" He jumps up. "It's not like you can tell her why."

"Yeah, but—"

He holds his hands up. "Seb, you can't. Do you want everyone to know? You can't trust this woman. You don't know her."

"I'd like to get to know her."

"Seb, come on, shut down the hormones for a second," he says. "Do you want your family to find out in the media?"

I ignore him and head out to my car. He follows me.

"Seb—"

"It's my understanding that she's paid to keep her clients out of the media," I say, still not turning around.

"You're not her client." He grabs my shoulder. "The Randalls are."

I spin around. "You think Gary Randall's going to let that

leak to the media? Really? He's going to take down his franchise player?"

"I think—strike that, I know—Gary's going to do whatever he needs to do to make himself and his family look good and turn a profit while he's doing it." He pauses, letting out a long breath. "I've worked for him for fifteen years—long before you got here. I know how he operates."

"Does Gary know I'm the one who asked for Liza to be removed?" I lower my voice as a few reporters walk by.

"I don't think so. Ken's sticking to our story," Joe whispers. "I'm wondering if Liza might have told Gentry, though. They're thick as thieves."

"Gentry's not going to say anything, even if he knows. He wants to be my best friend. He's more fanboy than owner."

Joe shakes his head as he walks toward his car. "Don't try to lose me at a light like you did yesterday."

Last season, a fan tried to get into my car when I was at a stoplight. Since then, the team makes Joe follow me everywhere.

"I didn't try to lose you. You're just getting old and slow."

"I'm about to show you old and slow," he says as he opens his door. "Hey. Just leave Sophie alone. Keep it on a professional level. She'll be out of here before we know it. It's what's best for everyone."

"Yeah, you're probably right," I say as I get into my car.

I grab my phone and stare at it for a second. She hasn't texted me yet. That's probably a good thing, but it sure doesn't feel that way right now.

"Where are the kids?" I walk out on my back deck to find Stone sitting alone, staring out at the bay.

I rent a five-bedroom/six-bathroom house on an island off Miami Beach. I use about a tenth of the space, but it's the only place I can get any peace. There's one entrance onto the island and it has round-the-clock security. The only way someone could get to me is if they came by boat off Biscayne Bay. I'm sure someone will try at some point.

Stone nods his head out toward the water where I see Ricky and Paul struggling to stay standing on my paddle boards. They're way too far out, as usual.

"At least Ricky's wearing a life jacket this time. I'd like to send you guys back to Michigan alive tomorrow."

I grab a beer out of the refrigerator and stretch out on a lounge chair. The best part about this house is a full outdoor kitchen surrounding the pool. It has an enormous flat-screen TV hanging from one wall with speakers surrounding a plush seating area. When I'm here, I spend ninety percent of my time on this very chair.

"Yeah, I didn't even have to lecture him," Stone says, laughing. "Maybe when he hit his head on the board the last time, it knocked some sense into him."

"I wouldn't go that far."

He cracks open a fresh beer. "So, you ever get the nerve to leave a message for that woman from last night? I'm going to lose a hundred if you did, so I'm rooting against it."

I drain the rest of my beer. "Turns out I didn't need to leave a message. She showed up at the stadium today."

"What?" He spins his head around to me. "Is she stalking you or something?"

"I don't think so." I glance down at the bay just in time to see Ricky wiping out after trying a handstand on the board. His lifejacket pulls him back to the surface. He's laughing so I guess he's okay. "She's a PR consultant. The team hired her."

"Uh, that's more than a little suspicious. Don't you think?" His eyes narrow. "I mean, she's crawling all over you last night, then she just happens to show up at your work today."

"I don't know," I say, rubbing my eyes and letting out a frustrated grunt. "I think it's a coincidence, but Joe's in your camp."

"Stop thinking with your dick and you'll be in our camp, too," he snarls. "She's hot, but that behavior's shady as fuck."

"Don't hold back, man," I say, glaring at him. "Tell me exactly how you feel."

"Look, Seb." He stands up and whistles for Ricky and Paul to come in. "I know you think you're ready to get married—"

"You're married. Paul's married. Shit, Ricky's already been married and divorced."

He turns around and leans against the railing. "We're not Seb Miller. There are only so many women who would want to marry us. Every woman wants to marry you. I know it's hard, but you've got to keep your guard up until you find someone you can trust. And this girl—"

"Woman," I say sharply, "and her name's Sophie."

"Okay, the way *Sophie* has shown up in your life seems a little too convenient."

"Joe said her job is to find out who got Liza Murray kicked out of the clubhouse—"

"What the fuck, Seb?" He walks over to me and lowers his

voice. "You know that. And you still think she's a possibility?"

I stand up to get another beer. "She doesn't know it was me, and even if she finds out, she won't know why. You and Joe are the only people who know. I mean besides Dad."

"Know what?" Paul swings the deck gate open and walks in with Ricky on his tail.

"Know that he didn't have the balls to call that girl last night," Stone says, handing them both a beer, "so you assholes owe me fifty each."

"Come on, man." Ricky slaps the back of my head. "You're Seb-Fucking-Miller. How are you going wimp out on calling a woman? Call her right now."

"I don't have her number."

"You're worthless," Paul says, laughing. "You went all the way up to her hotel room and you didn't even get her number? Man, you're losing your touch. Let me be clearer. You've lost it. It's completely gone."

I shake my head as I grab my phone off the table to see who's texting me. I stop breathing for a second when I see the message.

"Everything okay?" Stone asks.

"Yeah, it's just Joe. You know he can't leave me alone for more than ten minutes at a time. Some bullshit promotion I have to do before the game tomorrow."

I look back at my phone and try to keep a smile from exploding all over my face.

It's Sophie. This is my number if you still want it.

Chapter Eleven

SOPHIE

When I walk into the hotel suite, Maisie's still where I left her this morning—in bed, buried underneath the blankets. All I see is wet hair mounded on top of her head in a messy bun.

"Did you even get out of bed today?" I kick off my shoes and crawl in with her.

Her eyes—still smudged with mascara—pop out of the blankets. "Barely. I went down to the pool with the girls for a few hours, but it got so hot. I couldn't take it."

"Are they still down there?" I say, sinking back into the mounds of pillows. It reminds me of the pillows on Seb's office bed. His blue eyes flash through my brain. I shake my head to try to get them to disappear.

"I think," Maisie says as she snuggles onto my shoulder. "They've been drinking all day. I can't hang anymore. Do you remember in college when we could recover from a hangover in a couple of hours?"

"I remember when you could. It's always taken me at least a day."

"Oh, sweetie," she says, squeezing my hand, "you have to be about ready to crash. How was your meeting?"

"Well, two things. First, I got the contract, and second, wait, what was it again? Oh yeah, my new client is the baseball team. Guess who I saw today?"

She shoots up so quickly that she almost falls off the bed. "What? Did you see Seb?"

"Yes, friend. I did," I say, throwing a pillow at her. "Why didn't you tell me who he was?"

"Oh my God!" She has a death grip on the pillow. "I didn't know your new client was the team. You never tell me who you're working for—"

"And I shouldn't have now. You can't tell anyone else."

She nods, her eyes wide. "So, did you talk to him? Did he recognize you?"

"Yes and yes, and he lied to the owners about knowing me so I wouldn't get fired. One of the stipulations of the contract is that I don't have a prior association with any of the players."

She peers over the top of the pillow—her eyes dancing. "How do they feel about future *associations*?"

"Mae, you know I don't have personal relationships with my clients during or after my work with them."

"Bullshit!" She throws the pillow back at me. "Roman's like your best friend—besides me, of course."

"Yeah, he slipped through somehow," I say, yawning, "but he's the only one."

"Well, since you've already made an exception for him, I

vote that you make another exception for Seb. He was so sweet to you last night."

"He was so sweet to me today. He let me take a nap in his office—"

"What?" She crawls over to me until she's inches from my face. "A nap *with* him?"

"No! Maisie! He knew I was hungover, so he told me to sleep it off—alone."

She squeals. "Oh my God! He's so into you. It's the cutest thing. He asked me for your number last night. I didn't give it to him. Did you?"

"No, he gave me his, though." I know I shouldn't say this next part. "He said 'just in case I need him.'"

"Oh, you definitely need him!" She claps her hands together. "Give me your phone. We're texting him right now."

Her hands are swarming around my body like two large gnats. I swat them away. "*We're* not doing anything. I'll text him if I need to professionally, but other than that, I won't."

"Wait, do you not find him attractive?" She gasps as she puts her hands over her chest. "Soph, he's like a Greek god. And he's so sweet and gentle."

She stops suddenly and takes a quick breath. "This isn't about Sam, is it? Sam's an asshole. I don't think Seb's like that at all. I know you have trust issues, but I think Seb's worth the risk."

"It's not about Sam—or my trust issues. Seb seems great and, yeah, he's beautiful, but I need to keep a professional distance."

"Until you're done working there, but then maybe." She

shrugs and crawls back under the blankets with me. "Maybe bring him to my wedding. That's only a few weeks away."

"Maisie!" Savannah's voice thunders through from the other room.

"Don't tell them." I tap Maisie's head as Savannah bursts through the bedroom door with Taylor, Cate, and Serena on her heels.

"Look who made it back alive!" Serena flings herself onto the bed and lands with a thud on my chest. She smells like a rancid mixture of beer and suntan lotion.

"Get off me," I say, pushing her to the floor. "How are you still drinking today?"

She looks up at me, laughing. "This is the first time I've been away from my kid for more than one night. I'm going to do all the drinking while I can. Are you two going out with us tonight? Or are you going to be old women?"

"I'm not leaving this bed until I have to go into work tomorrow." I pull the covers up to my face. Maisie snuggles up beside me.

"You have to work tomorrow, too?" Taylor whines. "You're so adult now. It's awful. But I guess your meeting went well, huh?"

"Very well," Maisie says in a flirty voice. "Didn't it, Soph?"

I pinch her leg under the blankets. "Yeah, it went fine. I got the contract, and I made it through the day without throwing up or passing out, so a banner day all around."

"And all this hangover for nothing." Savannah laughs. "You didn't win Truth or Tequila for the first time. I can't believe you couldn't get him to kiss you. Has that ever happened before?"

"Still hasn't happened," Maisie mumbles into a pillow. My eyes question her as she sinks lower into the bed—a mischievous smile forming on her lips.

"I need a nap," I say, closing my eyes. "I'm out for tonight."

"Whatever," Savannah says as she heads back into the suite's main room. Thankfully, the others follow her.

I pull the blankets over Maisie's head and sink down with her. "What do you mean 'still hasn't happened'?"

"He kissed you before he left the room last night—a gentle brush over your lips. It was sexy as hell."

"What? Maisie! Why didn't you tell me?" I cover my eyes. "Why didn't *he* tell me? He probably thinks I'm easy."

"I don't think there's any chance of that," she says, snorting. "You were at the absolute highest level of your high maintenance last night."

"I meant sexually easy, Mae. He probably thinks I'm a slut."

"I doubt that, although you were begging him to kiss you—"

"Ahh." I let out a long groan.

"You promised him you'd go to sleep if he kissed you and he did. It was more sweet than slutty."

"So, I blackmailed him into a kiss? Cool. Cool."

"He wanted to kiss you. Soph, it was so tender. The perfect first kiss."

"Yeah, except that I don't remember it!"

"Text him," she says, grinning. "Maybe he'll come over here tonight and give you a kiss you'll remember."

"I hate you," I say as I crawl out of bed. "I'm taking a hot bath in that huge, glorious tub, and when I get back here, there better be pizza and some kind of trashy show on TV."

"Done." She glances at my phone that's still on the bed.

"And I'm taking my phone with me," I say, snatching it away from her. "I'm changing my password. You're not going to text him on my behalf."

"Okay," she says, smiling, "but if you die and I don't have your password, who's going to clear all the bad stuff before your mom can see it?"

I stick my tongue out at her before slamming the door. It takes me about two seconds to get naked and in the oversized, clawfoot tub. I sink down into it as the hot, sudsy water starts rising around me. I close my eyes and try to clear my mind, but I can't stop thinking about Seb.

I grab my phone off the floor and flip through my contacts until I get to his number. I stare at it for a full three minutes before I start typing.

It's Sophie. This is my number if you still want it.

As I lay my head back on a rolled-up towel and start to get comfortable, I hear the phone ping. I grab it so fast that I almost dump it in the tub.

Oh, I definitely still want it.

79

Chapter Twelve

SEB

"Sophie!"

She doesn't see it and it's on a collision course with her head. I know he lobbed it at her on purpose. That pisses me off, but one problem at a time. I'm about a foot from her before she even registers my presence. She finally looks up from her phone as I wrap my arm around her to shield her with my body. I snag the ball just before it hits her.

"What the—" She looks up at me as I hold the ball in front of her face. She flinches like I'm trying to smack her with it.

"You might want to get your nose out of your phone and look up when you're walking on the field. Baseballs are flying everywhere during warm-ups."

She looks from the ball to me. "Wait, did that almost hit me? I didn't even see it."

"Yeah, I'm aware of that, Sophie. It almost hit you in the head." I reluctantly let her go. "Get your nose out of your phone."

"I was working." She holds up her phone like she's doing show and tell for her third-grade class. When she smiles at me, her head tilts a little bit. It's so cute.

I lower her arm to her side. "Work with your eyes up when you're on the field," I say, smiling back at her.

"Hey, asshole," I hear coming from behind me. "You want to throw me back the ball."

When I turn around, I see Marty Clarkson looking at me. We played a few months of minor league together. The team signed him for the rest of the season. He's a decent outfielder, but just a horrible human being. I walk over to him, slinging the ball between my hand and my glove.

"She's off limits," I say when I get closer. I'm squeezing the ball so hard that I'm a little surprised it's not crumbling in my hand. "If I see you trying to get her attention again, we're going to address that asshole comment. You understand me?"

"Nice to see you again, too, Seb," he says, laughing. "I didn't know she was yours."

I take another toward him—until I'm inches from his face. "She's not mine. She's definitely not yours. She belongs to herself. She's here to do a job—just like you. Treat her with respect."

"All right, Franchise. We're good. We're good," he says, backing up. "Remember we're on the same team here."

"I think you hit a nerve, Marty." I turn toward the opposing team's dugout to see Lance Buckley staring at me. "You hitting that, Seb? Good work if so. She's a mighty fine specimen of woman."

He nods his head toward where Sophie's standing. I keep my eyes fixed on him. "You going to try to steal a base on me

81

again tonight, Buckley? What are you now? Like oh and twenty against me? I'd think you would have learned your lesson by now."

He spits out a few sunflower seed shells. "Ah, I see. You can't close that deal, huh? Maybe I'll take a shot at her after the game tonight. I'd like to peek under that little dress she's almost wearing."

"Keep talking, Buckley," I say, turning toward our dugout. "It's the only thing you do well."

I turn around to look for Sophie. She's not on the field anymore. It's probably better. I can't concentrate on anything except her when she's around. I need to get my head in the game.

"Seb." Bud, our manager, is jogging over to me. "Are you done warming up? You need to get off the field. Seb? What's wrong with you? Snap out of it. We've got a game to play."

When I walk out to take the field, I glance over to the owner's box seats. A wave of relief washes over me when I see Sophie sitting there. For some reason, I've started to feel like I need to know where she is before my brain can even function.

She's looking at me, a gentle smile on her beautiful lips. I have my mask on, but I nod slightly. Her smile gets bigger. She definitely saw the nod. I feel a rush of adrenaline shoot through my body.

God, she makes me hungry—hungrier than I've been in years. Just looking at her makes my heart beat faster. When I touch her, I feel like I'm about to explode. I can't even imagine what would happen if she let me kiss her or—

"Hey, Miller!" Dane yells at me from the pitcher's mound. "You want to get behind the plate or do you want me to throw to the ump tonight?"

I look at Sophie one more time before I take my place for the top of the first. After we get a quick two outs, Lance Buckley walks to the plate. He's their toughest out. He almost always finds a way to get on base. He works a count like no other player I've ever seen.

Buckley takes a called strike and then fouls one off. Dane has his slider working. It's a tricky little bastard when it's moving right, and it's moving just right tonight. I call for it again. Dane shakes me off. He wants to throw his heater, even though Buckley has owned it all season.

Dane's the most stubborn person I've ever met. I've caught every one of his games this season. He's 15-2—his best season by far—but he still feels like he can tell me what he wants to pitch. I call for the slider two more times. He shakes me off. Fine. Throw your fastball. Let's see how far Buckley can hit it this time.

The fastball comes in chest high. Buckley slaps it to right field for a single. I call for the ball from the cutoff and walk out to Dane.

"He hits your fastball every time, dumbass." I toss the ball back to him. "He's going to try to take second on the first pitch. Throw your heater low and then get the fuck out of my way."

Buckley's got a huge ego and absolutely no common

sense. After our exchange before the game, I know he's itching to run on me.

Dane throws the perfect pitch—low and away—and then hits the deck. I see Buckley take off out of the corner of my eye. I throw a rocket to our shortstop who's waiting for Buckley as he slides in. He's out by a mile. I throw my mask up and take a few steps toward the visiting dugout as Buckley walks that way. He keeps his head down.

"Say something about her again and it's going at your head," I growl as our third baseman jogs over to me.

"You got some extra juice tonight, Seb?" he says, pushing me back toward our dugout. "Keep it on the field, man. We need you in the game."

As I walk back to the dugout, I glance up at Sophie. She's still looking at me—smiling. Yeah, I definitely have some extra juice tonight.

Chapter Thirteen

SOPHIE

Seb just threw out a runner at second to end the inning. It was so hot. I'm not sure that's the correct reaction to a baseball play, but it's the one I had. I started sweating when I saw how hard he threw the ball. And I'm pretty sure the look he gave me as he walked back to the dugout almost burned the dress right off my body.

"Sophia?" Gary taps me on the arm.

"What?" I look at him and shake my head. "Sorry, I was in my own little world there."

"I asked you if you've made any progress on your assignment."

"Oh, not really. This is only my second day. I talked to a lot of the players today. None of them strike me as the kind of guys who would want a woman banned from the clubhouse—except maybe Dane. But he seems more like a harasser, less like a discriminator."

"What about Seb?"

His name makes me jump. "Uh, yeah, he doesn't seem much like the type to discriminate against anyone. Why? Do you think it was him?"

"I honestly don't know," Gary says, "but I think he's the only one with enough power over the PR staff to get it done."

I shift in my seat. "Why does he have so much power?"

"Because when I promised to pay him almost two hundred million over the next five years, I told everyone to treat him like a god. I want him happy because I want a return on my fucking investment."

Gentry's on my other side—listening intently but not talking. "What do you think, Gentry? Was Seb the one who got her kicked out?"

He sits up straight and leans back from me. "I don't know. Why would I know?"

He's a horrible liar. He knows. "It seems like you're plugged in with the players—like they trust you."

He smiles. Playing to a man's ego—especially one as stupid and arrogant as Gentry—works almost every time.

"Yeah, I think they do trust me, especially Seb, but he hasn't told me anything like that. I would have told Dad."

He looks over at his dad. Gary's talking to one of the other owners.

"I have to use the bathroom," Gentry says, glancing at me before he walks to the tunnel.

I wait for him to come back, but he never does. By the end of the third inning, I'm done chatting up the owners. I excuse myself to head to the press box. I barely get into the tunnels beneath the stadium when I hear my name.

"Sophia Banks?"

I turn around to see Liza Murray jogging down the concourse to catch up with me. She smiles and extends her hand. "I understand you're here to investigate my sexual discrimination claim."

I return her smile. "Oh yeah? Who told you that?"

"Gentry." She laughs as she adjusts her cell phone so it's on top of her notebook. I'm guessing the recorder's on.

"It was my understanding you had a do-not-discuss agreement with the Randalls."

"A handshake agreement." She smiles warmly again. "I would never sign something like that, and even if I did, Gentry's never met a non-disclosure agreement that he didn't bust through like the Kool-Aid man."

"Somehow," I say, laughing. "I believe that's very true."

"You know, you could save a lot of time if you asked me what happened."

My defensive shield shoots back into place. "Thank you for the offer, but I signed a non-disclosure. I don't feel comfortable talking to you on or off the record about this."

"Oh," she says, her face tightening, "so you're one of those, huh?"

"I'm not sure what you mean."

"One of those women who support the patriarchy because they let you have a seat at the table."

"I'm definitely not one of those." I'm trying to make my face look normal, but I can tell that my "fuck you" smile has spread across it.

"We'll see." She steps closer to me and lowers her voice. "Between us, watch out for Seb Miller."

I take a step back. "Why's that?"

"I see the way he looks at you. Don't feel bad, though. It's not your fault. Let's just say, we've all had that target on our backs."

"Good to know." Despite the disappointment surging through my body, I somehow manage to keep smiling.

"You know if you want to grab a drink or something some-time, I'd love that," she says, slipping her phone back in her pocket. "There aren't a lot of women to pal up with around here. Completely off the record. No professional talk at all."

"I appreciate the offer, but I separate my personal life from my professional life. It's the only way I can function."

She laughs. "Believe me, I understand. Just make sure that applies to Seb. He's a sneaky one."

My mind's spinning as she walks away. Seb's the last person I expected to be a part of this mess. He doesn't seem like the type at all, but she did say he was sneaky.

Seb's making a beeline over to me as I head to the clubhouse after the game. He just came off the field. He's already taken off his jersey. I'm guessing some kid got it after the last pitch. Ken told me he does that most nights.

His white undershirt's soaked with sweat. It's clinging to his chest—outlining every beautiful muscle. His hair's drenched, too, and jutting out in all directions. He's dirty and messy and just sexy as hell. I take a deep breath and close my eyes, letting Liza's warning fill up my body.

"You trying to work up enough courage to come into the clubhouse?" Seb's laughing as I open my eyes.

"What? No, I'm good." I try to walk around him, but he grabs my shoulder.

"Have you ever been in a clubhouse after a game?" he whispers. "Guys are in various states of dress—"

"Nothing I haven't seen before." I shrug his hand off.

His eyebrows shoot up. "All right," he says, laughing. "I didn't realize you were that, uh, experienced."

"What? No, I mean, I've seen them in limited q-quantities," I stutter. "Like I haven't seen a lot—of them. I mean enough, but—"

"Soph," he says, patting my back. "You're good."

He's trying to hold in a laugh. When he does that his eyes sparkle. It was endearing until my conversation with Liza. Now, it's annoying.

"Do you not want women in the clubhouse or something?" I cross my arms and stare at him.

"What? Where did that come from?" He has that hurt, puppy-dog look again. Unfortunately, that's still very endearing. "I was just giving you a heads-up. Uh, no pun intended."

I scowl as I walk around him. "You better not have intended that pun."

"I didn't!" He runs around me to open the door. "I swear. I'm sorry if it offended you."

"It only offended me because it's a pun. I hate puns." He's smiling again when I look back at him. "Seriously, Seb. They're the worst."

"Okay, okay. Noted. No puns ever again—intended or

unintended." He follows me in. "Did something happen? Your sass-level is off the charts right now."

"My *sass-level*," I say, not looking back, "is right where it needs to be."

Chapter Fourteen

SEB

"Put something on, asshole." I grab a towel as I walk out of the shower and throw it at Dane who's strutting through the clubhouse buck-ass naked. Sophie's sitting across the room talking to our newspaper beat reporter, Ray Franklin.

"Why? You getting turned on, Seb?" Dane flings the towel back at me. "And since when do you come out of the shower with your boxers and T-shirt already on? Is there someone in here who you don't want to see the goods?"

This is the first time I've ever come out of the shower wearing anything other than a towel. It's definitely because Sophie's in the room. I mean, I want her to see all of me, but I was hoping for a more intimate setting.

Dane walks over to Sophie and Ray. "You got any questions for me tonight, Ray?"

Sophie turns around to see his naked crotch right in her face. I grab Dane by the arm and throw him across the room. "Put some damn clothes on," I say, blocking Sophie's view.

"Why? I can't walk around free and easy because there's another woman in the room now?"

"Walk around how you want," I growl, "but you don't need to get that close to her."

"He does if I'm going to see anything," Sophie says from behind me. "It's kind of small."

"Oh!" The clubhouse erupts in laughter.

"Good one, Sophia." Manny, one of our pitchers, walks by and gives her a fist bump. He turns to Dane. "It is hard to see. Is it shy? Maybe it's hiding somewhere."

Dane flips him off and heads toward the shower. I turn back around to Sophie.

"Sorry about that. He's an asshole."

"Can I quote you on that?" Ray smiles at me. I know he won't. He's a good guy and a solid reporter. He's an old-school journalist. He doesn't spend time on clubhouse drama like some of the other reporters do.

"Sure. It's not like it's going to be breaking news or anything. You've been around long enough to know what Dane's like."

He laughs as he turns back to Sophie. "Is that the kind of sexual harassment you're here investigating?"

She looks up at me and then looks back at Ray. "I'm not sure what you're talking about, Ray."

"C'mon, Sophia. You've only been here a few days, but I'm guessing you've already figured out that this place is as leaky as a colander. Everyone knows what you do for a living. It's not that hard to figure out why you're here."

She glances at me again. She didn't want me to hear that. I'm beginning to think Joe might be right about her, but for some reason, it doesn't bother me at all. I want her to know everything about me—even the bad stuff.

"Off the record," she says, turning back to Ray.

"Sure."

"I'm not here about sexual harassment. It's the sexual discrimination stuff. You've seen the stories. You even reported on it."

"What Dane just did looked more like harassment to me." Ray nods toward the showers.

"I'm not talking about Dane and his little penis parade—"

"Oh God," Ray groans. "Can we please go on record just for that last statement? I've got to quote 'little penis parade.'"

"No, we cannot," she says, laughing, "but if you ever write a book, feel free to use that as the title."

"That's a best seller, right there," he nods and looks around the room to make sure no one's listening. "So you're here for the Liza Murray thing? That someone asked for her to be removed from the clubhouse?"

I'm trying to act uninterested as I get dressed at my locker, but I'm not doing a very good job.

"I'm here to make sure the organization's putting its best foot forward in every area which includes rooting out discrimination of any kind."

"Damn." Ray whistles. "You should run for office with that answer."

"Hey, Seb." I turn around to see Liza walking over to me. "I've got a few questions."

Ken steps in between us. "Liza, you know Seb doesn't answer questions until he's dressed. Give him a few minutes."

"And you know reporters work on deadlines, right?" She

laughs as she backs up a few steps. "And it's not like I haven't seen everything Seb has to offer many, *many* times before."

Sophie jumps up. "Nice talking to you, Ray," she says, shaking his hand. "I think I'm going to call it a night."

She glances back at me as she walks away. The way she looks at me has changed in the last few hours and not for the better. I'm going to have to get into that, but not here. I grab my phone and send her a text.

What's wrong?

"Sophia," Ray says to her back. "Any time you want to go on record, you know where I am."

She nods at him and then looks down at her phone. She takes a quick look at me again and puts the phone in her pocket without answering.

"Something going on there, Seb?" Ray's holding his phone out toward me.

"Naw, I don't mess with women who work here."

"Even when they look that good?" He lets out a slow whistle as he pulls out his notepad and pen.

"Especially then." I zip up my jeans and turn toward the gaggle of reporters pacing behind me. "You got any questions about the game, Ray? Or are you working for the *National Enquirer* now?"

"I'd probably get paid better if I worked for them," he says, chuckling. The other reporters start to circle me as Ray continues, "Yeah, why don't you tell me about that final out in the top of the first? I've never seen you throw that hard, and that's saying something. Did Buckley do something to piss you off?"

"Yeah, he got on base," I say, shaking my head. "You remember how this game works, right?"

———

When they built the new team parking garage at the stadium, they attached it to the front offices. Now the players have to walk by all the team's employees when we're going to and from the field. Gary Randall thought it would make us a more cohesive organization. The players hate it. Some of the staff are cool, but most of them are more annoying fans than the people who wait for us outside the stadium.

For the first couple weeks we parked there, staff members would take pictures of us and ask for autographs as we walked through the offices. We complained to our union, and that part finally stopped, but they still stare at us when we walk through. Tonight's no different, except for this time, I'm returning the stares—looking for Sophie. I texted her again without a response.

"Hey Barkley," I say to one of the sales guys. He's cool. The first thing he told me when we met was that he was more of a hockey guy. I respect that. "Do you know who Sophia Banks is?"

"Yeah, she already left. Consultants never stick around to do the dirty work, you know?" He laughs as he points to a table of promotional T-shirts that he and three other guys are folding.

"All right, thanks."

"Good game, Seb," one of the other guys says. "Solid hitting, but your timing seems off with the curve. Maybe start swinging a little earlier."

"Thanks for the tip," I say, glaring at him as I walk toward the parking garage door. Joe's already there, holding it open for me.

"I see you're still sniffing around after Sophie. I thought we agreed to leave her alone."

"I didn't agree to shit."

"Seb—"

"Joe, seriously, back off," I say, spinning around. I lower my voice as a few people look over. "Look, man, you've become a good friend to me, but it's important you know that I've knocked my friends to the ground more than once. I heard you. Now back off."

He stares at me and finally nods. "Roger that."

Chapter Fifteen

SOPHIE

Gary called me last night to invite me to New York with the team for the weekend. I didn't want to go, but here I am this morning—on the team's chartered plane—waiting for takeoff.

Most of the team's filed by me on the way to their private area in the back of the plane, but I haven't seen Seb yet. He texted me one more time after I left the clubhouse last night. I guess he got the hint when I didn't text back. I haven't heard from him since.

My conversation with Liza set off a warning bell in my head that I was losing objectivity where Seb's concerned. I need him to leave me alone so I can get this job done and get the hell away from this team before I make any mistakes.

I'm thinking about how I can most efficiently do that when I see Seb walk onto the plane followed, as always, by Joe. Seb's wearing jeans, a white, button-up dress shirt, and a blue, herringbone blazer. His hair's a little damp and slicked back, like he just washed it. There's one little curl that's escaped onto his forehead. He has a pair of aviator sunglasses hanging from the front of his shirt. He looks like he should be walking down a runway in Milan. If I weren't already sitting, I think I would faint just from looking at him.

After Seb hands his jacket to the flight attendant, he surveys the front cabin until he sees me. When his eyes lock with mine, I duck down behind the seat to hide from him—like a complete idiot. I grab earbuds out of my bag. Just as I get them in, I see Seb out of the corner of my eye, stopping at my seat. I'm desperately trying to ignore him by scrolling through the song library on my phone.

I act like I don't hear him say my name twice. He finally taps my arm. I look up, acting surprised. "Oh, hey," I say, taking an earbud out.

"Oh, hey," he says, smiling. "I asked if I could sit with you."

"Uh." It's all I can think to say. I'm usually a lot smoother than this, especially in business, but he's got me so flustered.

He sits down. "I'll take that as a yes."

Joe looks from him to me. He glares at me for a second before he heads to the back.

I start to put my earbud back in, but Seb catches my hand and lowers it. "You want to tell me what's changed in the last twenty-four hours?"

"What? What do you mean?" I can't hold his stare. "Nothing's changed."

"You're a really bad liar." I look up at him again. His eyes aren't blinking.

"Look, Seb," I say, taking a quick breath. "I told you the

first day that I can't have relationships with my clients—or their employees."

"I'm trying to be your friend—nothing more."

I raise my eyebrows and tilt my head. "You're a really bad liar, too."

He nods and laughs. "Yeah, I guess I am, but—"

My phone rings. It's Roman. He tried to call me once already this morning. He worries if I don't answer.

"Hold on," I say to Seb as I put my earbud back in and answer. "Hey. I can't talk long. I'm on a plane, getting ready to take off."

"Are you with the team?"

"Yeah."

"How's that going?"

"Fine."

"Are you okay?"

"Yeah."

"Sophia!" he yells. "Say the word pineapple if you're being held against your will."

"I'm not being held against my will," I whisper. I hear Seb laugh beside me.

"Then do you want to maybe answer me with more than one word at a time?" Roman's voice lowers when he's getting concerned. It's left his usual baritone range and is quickly falling deep into a bass. "And why are you whispering? And your voice sounds shaky? What's wrong?"

"Nothing's wrong. I'm good. Really."

"Soph," Roman says. His voice gets a little softer. "Are you worried about the hurricane?"

I sit up straight and jerk back away from the window. "What? What hurricane?"

"That's why I'm calling you. We just got back from St. John. It's supposed to hit there tomorrow, and it looks like it's headed this way. You need to start watching the news more."

I'm deathly afraid of hurricanes. I was just out of college when Hurricane Irma came through Miami. As Chicagoans, Maisie and I didn't have enough sense to evacuate from our beachside apartment. Luckily, Irma went a little north of the city, but I still remember the horrible, deafening sound of the wind. We huddled together in a closet and cried all night.

"When's it supposed to be here?" My voice shakes despite my efforts to keep it calm.

"By the weekend, honey, but if it looks like it's going to be a direct hit, you can hunker down with us at our house. You know it's like a fortress."

"Okay," I whisper.

"Soph, we'll take care of you. We always do."

"I know. I have to go. The flight attendant's staring at me."

"Okay, call me when you get back in town. We love you, Soph."

"I love you, too." I take a deep, shaky breath as I end the call.

"Is Roman your new boyfriend?" I jump when I hear Seb's voice right next to me. When Roman started talking about the hurricane, I forgot about everything else.

"Stop creeping on my phone." I grab it off my lap and slide it between my leg and the armrest.

"I wasn't creeping. It was sitting right there."

I look up at him. The sad eyes are back. I swear he could

get me to do just about anything with that look. "Roman's one of my best friends. He and his husband are like family. They take care of me."

"And protect you from things like hurricanes?" He pats my leg. The warning bell goes off again.

"You were eavesdropping?" I swat his hand away and scowl at him. "Stop it."

"Sophie, when you said 'hurricane,' your voice was almost too high for even dogs to hear. And you lurched back so far that you almost knocked me off the seat. Are you scared of hurricanes?"

"Isn't everyone scared of hurricanes?"

"Yeah," he says. "I guess sensible people anyway, but not much to do about them except get out of their way."

"Roman said I could stay at their house if it's supposed to be a direct hit."

He nods his head. "Yeah, or I'll take care of you."

"I don't need anyone to take care of me." Just as I say it, the plane hits some turbulence as it takes off. I grab the armrests and close my eyes tightly.

"Really?" He puts his hand on top of mine. "Breathe. Stop holding your breath, Sophie. The plane's fine."

"I'm okay," I whisper.

"Hmm. So, you're scared of hurricanes and air turbulence. Anything else?"

"Everyone should be scared of those things." I look down at his hand. It's still on top of mine.

"You're going to break the armrest if you don't relax your grip a little bit." He starts massaging my hand, trying to pry my fingers off.

I know I should move his hand, but as the plane continues to shake, it feels nice right where it is.

"Do you want me to move my hand?"

"Yes," I say, still looking at it, "but also no. And that's a perfectly legitimate answer."

He smiles. "Okay, I'm going to honor the 'no' for right now, but if you start leaning toward 'yes' just move my hand. No need to knock me to the floor this time, okay?"

"No promises."

He laughs and shakes his head. "You're a really confusing mix of fierce and sweet."

"They're not mutually exclusive. I can be both."

"And you definitely are. I'm just never sure which one I'm going to get."

I shrug. "Yeah, you know, right back at you. You have a lot of alpha-male bullshit going on, but you can be really sweet, too."

"If by 'alpha-male bullshit' you mean that I'm protective, yeah, I'm definitely protective of the people I care about, and that's starting to include you."

"Seb—"

"No," he says, squeezing my hand one more time before he lets it go. "You can't tell me who to care about. You don't have to return it, but I care about you. For some reason, it started the second I met you. That doesn't happen a lot."

"I talked to Liza Murray yesterday," I say, not looking at him.

He takes a deep breath. "I thought maybe that was it. Did she tell you I was the one who asked that she be removed from the clubhouse?"

"No, but I figured you were. She told me to watch out for you."

His jawline tightens. "I did ask for her to be removed, but not for the reasons you think."

"What reasons do I think?"

"Well, it damn sure wasn't because she's a woman. C'mon, Soph. I'm not that guy. I don't care about any of that. If people can do the job, they can do the job. It doesn't matter what sex they are."

"Then why did you ask for her to be removed?"

He rubs his hands over his face. "I can't tell you. I wish I could, but I can't."

I sink down in the seat and whisper, "Did you sleep with her?"

He spins his head back to me. "No! God, no. Seriously?"

"Well—"

He puts his hand up to stop me as he sinks down to my eye level. "Look, I know we just met, but you have to trust me. I was the one who asked for her to be removed. You can tell anyone you want. I don't care anymore. If it makes me look like an asshole, fine. The team can trade me if it's that big of a deal. I'm not worried about what they think of me, but I do care what you think. I'm not sexist. I didn't sleep with her. I had a good reason, but I can't tell you why. I hope you can trust me. Or at least quit looking at me like I'm the devil. Can we get back to a friendlier tone?"

"Yeah," I say, nodding. "Thanks for telling me you were the one who made the request. It makes my job easier. Maybe I can wrap this up earlier than I thought."

"Good. And maybe after you quit working here, you'll start returning my texts."

I turn toward him. His face is inches from mine. His eyes have turned hungry. They're fixed on my lips. He's so close I can feel his breath on my face. As his exhales turn into soft pants, I feel a tingling sensation spread between my legs.

"We'll see," I manage to get out before I sit up and turn quickly toward the window again.

Chapter Sixteen

SEB

"Heads up!" I say as I toss the ball to Sophie. She's walking toward me across the infield as we're wrapping up practice. She squeals and throws her hands over her eyes. The ball hits her on the hip.

"What was that?" I laugh as I bend over to pick up the ball.

"Don't throw balls at me." She frowns as she shoves me on my shoulder.

"I didn't throw it at you. I tossed it."

"Well don't toss it at me either." She's looking at the ball like it's her mortal enemy.

"What? Are you scared of a baseball?"

"No." She throws her shoulders back and tries to look insulted.

"Sophie." She recoils again when I hold the ball up to her face. "You flinched when I threw my keys to you in my office that first day. I thought you were just in a hangover haze. Are you scared of things being thrown at you?"

"No!" She tries to keep eye contact with me. "Maybe."

"Okay," I say, trying hard not to laugh. "Why are you scared of things being thrown at you? Did you get hit in the head when you were a kid or something?"

Her cheeks start turning pink. "Yes, and they did it on purpose," she says, crossing her arms.

"Who threw something at your head on purpose?" I'm somehow still managing not to smile. Her face is so serious.

"Don't make fun of me." She shoves me again. "It was my big brothers when I was like five. They threw a Nerf football at my head, and they haven't stopped throwing stuff at me since then."

"Do you want me to kick their asses?"

"Yes!" She nods her head vigorously. "Repeatedly."

"Okay, I promise I'll kick their asses, but in the meantime, let's teach you how to catch."

She leans back like I tried to slap her. "No!"

"Sophie, you need to learn how to catch things for normal life—like when someone tosses you your keys or your phone."

"Why does anyone need to throw things at me?" Her brow furrows as she crosses her arms again. "Can they not hand them to me? We live in a civilized world, Seb."

I shake my head and sigh. "Sit down, Sophie. I'll teach you like I do for little kids."

She frowns at me as I plop down on the field.

"Here." I pat the ground in front of me. "Right in front of me—knees touching."

"Don't treat me like I'm five—"

"Stop acting like you're five. I'm not asking you to catch Manny's fastball. Sit."

She looks back at Joe who's hovering as usual. "What do you think, Joe?"

"I think that there are grown men who would pay thousands, if not hundreds of thousands, to play catch with Seb Miller."

"And there are women who would pay millions to touch his knees." Our shortstop, Alex, walks over. "Soph, after he teaches you how to catch, I'll teach you how to field a grounder. Seb couldn't do that if I slow-rolled it to him."

"You better keep those eyes wide open the next time you cover second," I say, looking up at Alex. "My arm's feeling a little wild."

"All right, all right," Alex says, laughing, "I'll leave you to your playtime."

"Sophie, sit." I point to the ground again. "Now."

"Control issues!" She points at me.

"Oh, he definitely has control issues," Dane says as he walks over. "I've never met a catcher who doesn't though."

"If I didn't manage what pitches you throw, you wouldn't have any wins. Complain about my control issues when you get a fucking Cy Young nomination."

"I'm not complaining. Sophie, let him teach you how to catch and then I'll teach you how to throw a fastball."

Manny falls onto the field, laughing. "How are you going to teach anyone to throw a fastball? What'd they clock that pitch at the other night? Like seventy-two?"

"It was a called strike, asshole." Dane kicks him in the leg.

"Yeah because the batter was so confused about how slow

it was coming in," Alex says as he pulls Manny up off the field.

Dane nudges Sophie's shoulder. "Sometimes being controlled can be a good thing. You know what I mean?" he says, winking.

"Gross," she says. "Go away, Dane."

"Wowww," Dane says. "No woman has ever told me to go away."

"Oh, I'm one hundred percent sure that's not true," Sophie says.

"Okay," Dane says as he backs up and follows Alex and Manny off the field—his arms spread wide. "You don't know what you're passing up."

"Oh, I do," Sophie says. "Remember? I've already seen everything you have to offer. Pass."

He flips her off as he disappears into the dugout. I'm going to have to break that finger after the season's over. Sophie turns around and scowls when she sees me still sitting on the field.

"Sophie," I say. "Please sit down so you can learn how to catch. Being scared of hurricanes is one thing, but none of my friends are going to be scared of catching."

"Are we friends, Seb?" she says, smiling.

"For now." I pat the ground in front of me again. "Let's see how this goes."

She finally sits down with an impressive amount of drama. "I don't want to learn how to catch."

"I know you don't, but you're going to anyway." She flinches again as I toss the ball a few inches in the air and trap it against my chest. "Trap it like that against your chest at first. Don't try to catch it with your hands."

I toss it at her chest. She throws her hands over her face. The ball hits her forearm.

"Okay, lesson one," I say, pulling her arms down. "You have to keep your eyes open."

"You're wearing a chest protector. It's not fair."

"The chest protector is for ninety-five-mile-per-hour fastballs, but you can wear it if you want."

She thinks about it for a second but then shakes her head.

"Okay, I'm going to throw it so gently. I promise. Keep your eyes open."

"I don't want to."

"I know you don't, but you're going to anyway. Trap it against your chest like I showed you. I won't get it anywhere near your head."

I toss it again. She squints but manages to keep her eyes open and catch it against her chest.

"Good! That was perfect."

"Don't make fun of me!" she says, laughing as she tosses the ball back.

"I'm not. I promise." I scoot back a foot. "And that was a really good throw. It's the best pitch I've caught in weeks."

"Shut up." She frowns at me, but I can see a smile forming at the corners of her mouth.

I hold the ball out toward her. She doesn't flinch this time. Progress. "Will you try to catch it with your hands this time? Keep your eyes open and on the ball the entire time."

She nods her head and locks her eyes on the ball. She's concentrating so hard. I suppress another laugh and toss the ball. She straightens her arms and catches it way out in front of her body.

"That was good, but don't catch it so far in front. Let it come into your body. Throw it to me. See how I let it come to me. Let's try it again."

"Good." I keep scooting back a foot at a time until I get about ten feet from her. "Okay, let's try it standing."

She stands up and starts shifting nervously.

"Soph, it's the same as sitting. Just keep your eyes on the ball the whole time. Okay? Let it come into your body. You ready?"

I toss it a little too high. She twists her body, but somehow still manages to catch it.

"That's perfect. Good adjustment," I say, nodding. "Ken, grab her a glove."

Ken walks over to her with the ball boy's glove. "I've worked here ten years and I've never once got to play catch with any of the players, much less Seb Miller. Cherish this."

She looks up at me as I walk back to her. She smiles—her eyes lighting up a little. I think she might be starting to trust me again.

"Let's try catching with the glove." I throw the ball up and squeeze it as it lands in my glove. "Squeeze the glove around it like that—like a shark gobbling it up."

She laughs. "Is that what you tell kids? About the shark?"

"Depends on the kid. Sometimes it's dinosaurs. You seem like more of a shark person."

We spend about twenty minutes tossing the ball back and forth until she can catch it in the glove from about ten feet.

"I'm proud of you, Soph. You learned that so quickly," I say as I motion her ahead of me to the dugout.

"You're a good teacher," she says, smiling at me. She's back to looking at me with that soft glow in her eyes that mesmerized me the night I met her.

I put my hand on her shoulder. "So, let's see, we've solved your catching problem and I know that distraction is the key to your hurricane and air turbulence phobias. Are you scared of anything else?"

"Yeah, toothpicks," she says, her face scrunching up. "There was one in my sandwich when I was like eight years old. I didn't see it and it got stuck in the roof of my mouth. Why do they have to be so pointy?"

"Truly one of life's great mysteries."

She laughs as she hops down the stairs into the dugout. "My brothers are going to be so surprised the next time they throw something at me, but I still want you to kick their asses."

"Understood. It's the first thing I'll do when I meet them."

Chapter Seventeen

SOPHIE

Ray smiles at me as I slide into the chair next to him in the press box. "I saw you playing catch with Seb this afternoon. I've never seen him do that with anyone except kids."

"Well, I catch like a kid, so that's probably why he did it."

"Yeah," he says, raising his eyebrows, "that's probably why. I can't think of any other possible reason."

I ignore him. "Hey, I need to go off the record with you again."

He sighs. "That seems to be where we're living, Sophia. You know I literally get paid for putting things on the record."

"I know, but I'm not there yet."

He shakes his head. "Fine."

"I need to hear you say it—that we're off the record," I whisper.

"I've been doing this job for three decades. I'm not some damn hack. When you say off the record, it's vaulted."

I nod. "Seb was the one who asked that Liza be removed from the clubhouse."

He looks at me for a second and then turns his attention back to the field. "Yeah, I figured. He's the only one with enough clout to get it done."

"What do you mean?"

"Ken, and the entire PR staff, worship the ground that Seb walks on. They'd do anything for him even if it meant getting some flack for it. Anyone would do anything for Seb. He's a good guy."

"If he's such a good guy, why'd he ask for her to be removed?"

Ray marks another out on his scorecard. "I don't know," he says, looking back at me, "but I don't think it's anything major. She probably wrote something questionable about him."

"I've read everything she's written in the last few years. There's nothing questionable. She's a solid writer."

"Yeah, she can put a sentence together," he says, "but her ethics are a little questionable."

"How?"

"Well, she got fired from the paper around the same time this all started bubbling up." He peers over the top of his glasses at me for a second before he continues. "I've never known exactly why she got fired, but I have some ideas."

"You think she slept with Seb?"

"What?" he says, laughing. "No. That did not happen. I've seen who Seb dates. You're more his type than she is."

I frown at him. "Meaning?"

"Seb doesn't like the skinny, boney type. He likes a little heft."

I choke on the water I'm drinking. "Did you just call me hefty?"

"I absolutely did not." He holds his hands up and leans back away from me. "Not the best choice of words—"

"Ya think? Good thing you don't get paid for anything that involves word choice."

"I meant," he says, still laughing, "that you're, uh, how do I say this and keep it PC? Uh, you're put together nicely."

"Still not strictly PC, but right back at you, Ray. Don't think the ladies aren't looking when you walk away."

"Oh God, Sophia," he says, patting my hand, "you're good for this old man's soul. No one, except for my wife, has ever looked at my backside, and she hasn't done it in thirty years."

"I'm sure she still does. She's probably just sneaky about it," I say, smiling. "By the way, I didn't know Liza got fired. That's not the official story."

"It never is—"

"So why was she fired?"

"Like I said, I have some ideas, but I don't speculate, especially when someone's career might be affected."

"Huh. Well, I don't think Seb's sexist, and you say he didn't sleep with her, so what are they covering up?"

He pauses as another reporter walks behind us then lowers his voice. "If you're looking for the real cover-up, you might want to start with the man who hired you."

"Gary?" I whisper.

"And his son. Lots of talk there."

"What kind of talk?"

He puts his hand over his mouth and mumbles. "Some staff complaints."

"Complaints? Like what?" I swivel my head around to make sure no one's listening.

"The word is a few of the female staff have filed HR complaints that Gentry flirts inappropriately with them. I think he sees the team as a dating service instead of a working, professional office."

"I could see that," I say, nodding. "He flirts his ass off with me—sly innuendos, but still completely inappropriate stuff. Are you pursuing that as a story?"

"Maybe," he says, looking around again. "If you pair it with the Liza stuff, it's an office culture story. Maybe you can get me some sources and go on the record yourself."

"I think you know I'm paid to do the exact opposite of that."

"Yeah, I know what you do." He looks over his glasses at me again. "Look, I like you, Sophia. You seem like a good person, but I'm going to tell you, spinning some product recall is one thing, but spinning this type of behavior is a whole other thing. Once you take that step, I don't think you'll ever recover."

I nod but can't seem to come up with a reply. I know Gentry's a douche, but I didn't think it went any further than that. Gary certainly didn't tell me about any official complaints.

"Be careful, Sophia. Gary's obsessed with protecting his family's reputation," Ray says. "And now, if you're done distracting me, I should start paying attention to the game again before I get fired, too."

After I leave Ray, I'm thinking about heading back to the hotel early. My head's spinning. I need some time alone to sort through all of this. As I'm leaving the press box, I hear Gary's voice behind me.

"Sophia!" I turn around to see him standing at the door of one of the private luxury suites, motioning me inside. "I have some sponsors I want you to meet."

That's the absolute last thing I want to do, but since he's paying me, I guess I probably should. As I walk into the suite, there are people spread out all over the couches inside the air-conditioned area. Not one of them is watching the game.

"Sophia Banks, this is Matt Lowry—one of the team's largest sponsors."

"It's nice to meet you Mr. Lowry," I say, shaking his hand.

He holds my hand way too long. "It's my pleasure, Sophia, and please call me Matt."

Gary hands me a glass of wine. There's not a chance in hell I'm drinking any of it. I'm sure I'm probably overreacting, but these people are starting to give me the creeps.

"What kind of business are you in?" I say, trying to return Matt's smile.

"Sophia!" Gary turns to look at me—his eyes indignant. "Matt owns the largest fleet of private jets in Miami. How do you not know who he is?"

"I'm afraid I don't use private jets much. No offense, Mr. Lowry."

"It's Matt," he says, reaching out to clink my glass with

his. "And I'm going to have to get you up in one. You can be my special guest."

"Thanks, but—"

"I meant professionally, of course," he says. "I'm sure some of your clients use private jets. Gary said you work with the Miami elite."

"I don't talk about my clients," I say, putting my wine back on the bar. "I sign non-disclosures—"

"Matt knows what you're doing for the team," Gary interrupts. "We've already discussed it. He might have some work for you."

"Yes," Matt says, "I might have some *problems* in my company that you can help me with when you're done here. Let's talk about it at the client party after the game."

I look at Gary. "Client party?"

"We do one every time we get to New York. An after-party so the sponsors can rub elbows with the players. Stop by. It's in the main ballroom."

―――――――――

"Sophia, come over here and have a drink with me." Matt Lowry's holding up a bottle of wine when I walk into the ballroom.

"Oh, thank you, Mr. Lowry, but I don't mix drinking with business. I'm afraid I'm too much of a lightweight."

"Well, the only cure for that is drinking more," he says, smiling broadly. "And maybe if you have a glass of wine, you'll finally call me Matt. C'mon. Nothing serious. Just a friendly glass of wine so we can get to know each other a little better."

"I'm going to pass." I take a step back. The warning bells are going off again. "I don't mix business with personal either."

"Ah, I see." He pours himself another very full glass. "You're still young enough to think there's a difference between business and personal."

"I don't know if it has anything to do with age. It's more of a mindset."

He laughs. "You're too idealistic for someone who works in crisis communication. I'm sure you've seen some stuff."

"Some," I say, looking around the room. I'd rather be talking to just about anyone right now.

"Sit down, Sophia. Please. I'd like to discuss a business opportunity with my company."

"What business opportunity?"

He's patting the couch cushion next to him. I sit down in the chair the farthest away from him.

He laughs and shakes his head. "Gary tells me you're discreet about problems of a more, um, personal nature."

"I have no idea what that means. My job's to help companies identify problems, work through them, and then try to ensure that they don't happen again." I cross my arms. "I don't spin. I don't cover up."

"Ah, so very idealistic," he says. "It's a nice mission statement, but I wonder how many times you've stuck to it. Don't think everyone doesn't know what you're *not* covering up for Gentry."

Am I the only one who hasn't heard these rumors about

Gentry? I need to find out more about it, but I don't want to hear it from this guy.

"It's been nice talking to you," I say, standing up, "but my client list is full right now. If you'll excuse me, I think I'm going to call it a night."

He springs up. "I'll walk you to your room."

"The hell you will." I spin around to find Seb glaring at Matt.

Chapter Eighteen

SEB

"I hate this fucking party," I mumble to no one in particular.

"It's only once a season," Joe says from behind me. "These people pay your salary."

Every season when we're playing in New York, the Randalls throw a party for all the team's largest sponsors. The players are required by contract to be here. We hate it. It's usually after a game. We're tired and hungry, and we don't want to spend hours making small talk.

"Do they have any real food here this year?" I look around for a buffet table but don't see one.

"Naw, just appetizers." Joe grabs the waiter who's been circling me with a tray of food for the last five minutes.

The waiter holds up his tray. It's some kind of cheese and meat—each piece stabbed in the center with a toothpick. I smile as I think of Sophie. I scan my eyes around the room again but don't see her.

"These any good?" I look from the tray to the waiter.

He shrugs. "I don't eat this crap. You wouldn't either if you knew the people who prepare it."

"Good tip," I say, nodding. "Is that my rookie card sticking out of your shirt pocket?"

"Yeah," he says, looking over his shoulder, "but I'll get fired if I ask you to sign it."

I grab it out of his pocket and take a napkin off the tray. "Circle back around and pick up my napkin in a minute."

As I sign it, I see Gentry making his way over to me— dragging some other guy along with him.

"Seb," Gentry says, putting his arm around me. "This is Jeff Manning. He's a new sponsor."

"Hey." I shake Jeff's hand. Gentry's arm is still around me. I glare down at him. Joe pulls Gentry's arm away from me. I don't know how much the Randalls pay Joe, but it's not even close to being enough.

"Hey, Seb," Jeff says. "It's nice to meet you. I'm a huge fan. My son's an even bigger fan. He's a catcher, too."

The waiter circles back around. I lay the autographed baseball card—wrapped in the napkin—back on his tray. Gentry tries to grab a cheese thing, but the waiter's already halfway across the room, looking at the card. He turns around and gives me a discreet nod before he heads back into the kitchen.

"Oh yeah," I say, looking back at Jeff. "How old's your son?"

"Thirteen. You know, the asshole age. The only things that make him happy right now are baseball and looking at the sixteen-year-old girl who lives across the street."

"That sounds about right." I laugh. "Do you want an autograph for him?"

"Yes." He holds up a baseball. "But I'd really like a picture with you to show him that his dad is maybe even halfway cool."

"If my dad had come home with a picture of himself and Jorge Posada when I was that age, I would have been more pissed than impressed." Joe hands me a Sharpie to sign the ball. "There's no way to look cool to a thirteen-year-old."

"Yeah, that's the truth." Jeff hands his phone to Joe. "You were a Posada fan growing up?"

Joe motions for us to stand together and takes the picture quickly. He knows my patience level is low for stuff like this.

"Yeah, I worshipped him," I say. "Still do."

"You ever get to meet him?"

"Once. He was cool."

"So are you, man," he says, shaking my hand again. "I appreciate the picture."

"Let me know if it works with your son." I tap Joe and point at Jeff. "And tell him to write me if he wants any catching tips. I answer the stuff that comes to this address. Don't share it with anyone else."

He looks up at me—a stunned look on his face. "Really? Damn. I'm going to be the fucking father of the year after this."

As he walks away, I see Sophie walking into the room. She's barely through the door when some guy says something to her as he holds up a bottle of wine. She hesitates a few times before she finally takes a seat across from him.

"Gentry, who's that guy over there? The one sitting with Sophie."

"His name's Matt Lowry—one of our biggest sponsors. He owns a fleet of private jets."

"Good guy?"

"No, man, total dick," he says, grinning, "but most of us are. You know how it works when you get some money—it comes with some extra privileges. I'll introduce you so you have the hookup for his jets."

He grabs my arm and tries to pull me after him. I don't move. He looks back and drops my arm when he sees my face.

"I'll introduce myself," I growl. He takes a quick step back from me.

As I close in on Matt Lowry, Sophie stands up—her body's as rigid as a metal pole.

"It's been nice talking to you," she hisses, "but my client list is full right now. If you'll excuse me, I think I'm going to call it a night."

Lowry jumps up. "I'll walk you to your room."

"The hell you will," I say, closing the rest of the distance between us. I stand in front of Sophie.

Lowry laughs and shakes his head. "I've been coming to this party for three years and I've never even gotten close to meeting Seb Miller. Now, Sophia Banks graces my circle and you run right over here."

He holds out his hand. I think about giving him a quick right cross to the jaw until I feel Joe's hand on my arm, pulling me back.

"Sophie, I'll walk you to your room," I say, turning around without shaking Lowry's hand.

"Nope," Joe says, taking Sophie's arm. "I'll walk her to her room."

"You know, guys," Sophie says as she pulls her arm away from Joe, "I'll walk myself to my room because I'm an adult who has been walking for twenty years—"

"You've only been walking since you were six?" I say, raising my eyebrows and smiling.

"Shut up," she says, smiling. "I was rounding."

She turns toward the exit. I look back at Lowry. He's still eyeing her like a tasty snack. I know he's going to follow her if she leaves by herself.

"Soph." I start following her. Joe grabs my shoulder.

"Seb, I'm walking her. Stay here until I get back, and try to at least act like you're enjoying yourself," he says, pointing me to the group of players over in the corner. He turns to Lowry. "And Mr. Lowry, you enjoy the rest of that wine."

Joe smiles at him before he turns away. He's way better at hiding his feelings than I am. I'm going to have to get him to teach me how to do that. He looks over his shoulder as he follows Sophie out the door. He motions for me to start walking across the room. I nod and head over to the other players.

Chapter Nineteen

SOPHIE

Joe follows me out of the ballroom. Honestly, I'm glad he's walking me to my room. Guys like Matt Lowry are way too arrogant to take no for an answer.

"I know why you're here," Joe says as he catches up to me.

"In New York?" I glance back at him. His eyes are hard.

"I meant," he says, his voice getting gruff, "I know why you're working with the team."

I laugh. "Yeah, I'm finding out that almost everyone does. I've never worked at a place with so many leaks. That's probably part of the problem with the media."

He holds the elevator door open for me. "No matter what you've been told, Liza Murray is the problem—not one of the players."

"Seb told me he was the one who asked for her to be removed from the clubhouse."

He sighs and rubs his face. "That dumbass. I told him not to tell you. Are you going to tell Gary?"

"Yeah, probably." I shrug. "Seb doesn't seem to have a problem with it."

He shakes his head. "Seb wouldn't have a problem if you stuck an ice pick right in his eye. He's not thinking with his brain where you're concerned."

"Whatever," I say. "But bottom line, Gary's going to find out it was Seb eventually. And I'm not sure what the big deal is. I'm here because the media's saying the organization's sexist. If that wasn't why he asked for her to be removed, he just needs to tell everyone the reason."

Joe grabs my arm and glares down at me. "He's not going to tell anyone the reason. And that's why no one needs to know it was him. The story's going to cycle out like they all do. Keep your mouth shut until then."

As the elevator door opens on my floor, I pull my arm back and walk quickly out into the hallway. "Are you threatening me?"

"I'm not threatening you." He follows me off but stops walking when I hold up my hands.

"It sure sounded like that." I start backing away from him. I nod my head down the hallway. "My room's down there. I don't want you to walk me the rest of the way."

He takes a few steps away from me. "I'll watch you until you get inside."

"That's not necessary." I'm still backing toward my room. I don't want to take my eyes off him.

"It's necessary because if anything happens to you Seb will kill me."

"Funny because the only one I'm worried about right now is you." I swipe my keycard and slam the door behind me. I turn the deadbolt and lean against the wall. My head's spinning again.

My eyes dart around the room as I flip on the lights. I look in the shower, the closet, and under the bed. I know I'm alone, but I'm starting to get freaked out. As I dive into bed and pull the covers around me, I call Roman. He answers on speaker.

"Sophia!" he yells as a flurry of other voices say my name. There's loud music playing in the background.

"Roman, I need you alone," I yell to try to be heard over the din.

"Oh, Soph, I'm flattered, but you know I don't swing that way."

"I swing that way, Sophie." Roman's brother Carlos shouts. "I need you alone, too."

"If you swing your dick anywhere near her, I will cut it off," Roman growls at him.

"Roman!" I yell into the phone again. "I need to talk to you—alone."

He takes the phone off speaker. "Soph, what's wrong? I'm walking back to my office. Where are you? Are you okay?"

"I'm still in New York. I'm safe."

"What do you mean you're safe? Safe from what?"

I take a deep breath. "Things are getting weird. I need some information."

"What do you mean 'weird'?" His voice is getting deeper again.

"You insinuated that Gentry might be sexually inappropriate. Tell me exactly what you've heard."

"Sophie! Did he touch you? I swear to God I will fly to New York right now and tear him into tiny pieces."

"He hasn't touched me, and if he does, I'll flatten him. You know I can take care of myself. But he says inappropriate crap all the time. Just tell me what you know."

He takes a deep breath and whistles it out through his teeth. "I don't know anything for sure, but it's a pretty widely held belief that Gary's grooming him to take over the team but can't quite get there because female staff have complained about Gentry harassing them."

"What do you mean by 'harassing'? Like he said stuff to them or was it physical?"

"I don't know, Soph. Maybe some of each, but it's bad enough that the minority owners are blocking Gentry from being any more involved with the team."

When I don't say anything, he continues, "Soph, why don't you resign the contract? Come home now. I'll book you a flight or send my plane up for you."

"We're coming back tomorrow morning—"

"On the team plane? Where Gentry is? Hell no."

"The owners don't ride on the team plane. At least they didn't on the way up here. I'll be fine." I stop to think for a second before I reluctantly add. "Will you dig up some information on a guy named Joe Thomas? He works security for the team."

"What kind of information?" I'm not sure if there's a voice range below bass, but if there is, that's where Roman's at right now.

"I don't know. He rubs me the wrong way. There's something off there."

He growls into the phone again. "Sophia, do not leave your hotel room. I'm coming up there tonight to get you."

"No, you're not. I'm fine. Really, Roman. I'm good. You know I'd tell you if I wasn't."

Roman takes another deep breath. "Maisie told me Seb Miller's trying to get with you—"

"Oh my God! Why do you two talk?" I yell, throwing the phone away from me. "Seriously, she's not supposed to be sharing best friend information with you."

He ignores me. "She said she met him and he seems all right. She's a good judge of character. I trust her. If you have him watch your back until you get home, I'd feel a lot better."

"I'm not asking him to watch my back. He's the superstar. The team has people watching his back, and this Joe guy is one of them, by the way."

"Hmm. Hold on." I hear him yelling something but can't make out what he's saying. He must be covering the microphone. "I'm back."

"How's the hurricane?"

"Don't try to change the topic to something more agreeable, Sophia. I know how you operate."

"Roman," I whine. "How is a hurricane more agreeable than anything?"

"Well actually, this one is. It's going east of Miami—supposed to hit up around South Carolina. We should be fine."

"Okay, that makes me feel better at least."

"I'm worried about you, Soph. Call me when you're on the plane tomorrow."

"Okay." I'm a little surprised he's giving up this easily. He usually doesn't. "I'll be fine."

"Oh, I'm going to make sure of that," he says as he hangs up.

Chapter Twenty

SEB

When Joe got back to the ballroom and assured me that Sophie was safe, I headed back to my room. Since I've been here, I've gotten three calls from the same unknown number. I didn't answer them. I hear my text ping.

> *This is Sophie's friend Roman Garcia. I need to talk to you. Now.*

I call him immediately. He picks up on the first ring.

"Is this Seb?"

"Yeah. What's wrong with Sophie? Is she okay?"

"I just got done talking to her. I'm not sure what's going on," he says, "but I'd feel a lot better if you keep an eye on her until she gets back to Miami. Maisie seems to think you can be trusted."

My entire body tenses up. "Why does anyone need to keep

an eye on her? Is someone trying to hurt her? Do I need to go to her room right now?"

"No, she's good for tonight, but I wouldn't hate it if you met her at her room tomorrow morning and made sure she got to the airport safely."

I jump off the bed and grab my keycard. "I'll go camp outside her room right now, but you need to tell me a little more."

He doesn't say anything for a second. When he does, his voice has dropped into a low, menacing tone. "What do you know about Gentry Randall?"

"Nothing good. He's an asshole." I resist the urge to put my fist through the wall. "Did he do something to her?"

"Not yet."

"Do you know what room she's in? I'm not going to be able to sleep now. I'll get my security guy to watch her door."

"Joe?" His voice gets even lower.

"Yeah. Do you know Joe?"

He mumbles something that I can't understand. I hear someone else reply to him. "No, I don't know Joe, but Sophie has a bad feeling about him, too."

"What?" I start pacing. "He walked Sophie to her room tonight. Did he do something? There's no way. Joe's a good guy."

"I'll take your word for it. Look, Sophie's tough as nails. I've seen her take apart plenty of people verbally, and physically if she needs to, but I'd still feel better if you had her back."

"Nothing's going to happen to her," I say, my teeth clenched. "Trust me."

"I do. Don't let me down." He hangs up without waiting for a reply.

I call Ken. It takes him a few rings to answer. He must have been sleeping.

"What's up, Seb?" he says, yawning.

"What room is Sophie in?"

"What? Seb—"

"It's not what you think. Settle down. Just give me the number."

"Uh, hold on." I hear some papers rustling in the background. "324. If you're going to pay her a late-night visit, make sure Joe—"

"I'm not paying her a late-night visit. Get your mind out of the gutter." I pause for a second. "This is between us, Ken. Don't involve Joe. I'm serious."

"Seb—" I hang up before he has a chance to finish.

———

I texted Sophie after I hung up with Ken to make sure she got back to the room safely. She texted right back—like nothing was wrong. I didn't tell her about Roman's call. I couldn't sleep, so I wandered by her door a few times overnight to make sure everything seemed peaceful. At five, I decided to camp outside her door until she came out.

I finally hear her door opening. I jump up and stand to the side a little bit, so I won't scare her. It doesn't work.

"Jesus, Seb!" She falls against the door frame. "You scared the crap out of me."

"Sorry," I say, grabbing her rolling bag that's fallen out into the hallway. "I was waiting for you."

"What? Why? For how long?" She scrunches up her face. "What?"

"Your friend Roman called me last night—"

"Oh my God." She tries to grab the handle of her bag. I pull it farther away from her. "Roman's crazy. I'm fine."

"I think both of those things are probably true," I say, motioning her to go ahead of me toward the elevators, "but I'm here, so I might as well walk with you to the bus."

"What if someone sees us? They're going to think we spent the night together."

"No, they're not. We just happened to catch the same elevator. We're good." I hold the elevator open for her as I roll both of our bags in. "And if you didn't want Roman to call me, why'd you give him my number?"

"Are you insane? I would never give him your number. He's way too involved in my life already."

"How'd he get it then?"

She covers her eyes and shakes her head. "Roman has his ways. Believe me."

"Oh, I do. He sounded like someone who could get about anything he needed."

She looks at me through her fingers. "Just please delete his number and never answer another call from him."

"Hell no. I already saved it to my favorites and put him on speed dial."

"Seb—" She's cut off by the swarm of fans who rush the door when it opens in the lobby.

Joe plows a path right through them. "Where the hell have you been?" he says, grabbing my arm.

He glances at Sophie and then tries to push me through the crowd ahead of him. I don't move. I turn around and pull Sophie in front of me. She grabs her bag and starts walking toward the bus. I look back down at Joe. He's glaring at me.

"I'm not paid to protect her," he snarls.

"You don't have to protect her because I am." I glare back at him. "You want to tell me what happened when you walked her to the room last night?"

The rest of the security team has gotten to us. Joe looks up at me and nods toward the bus. I turn around and jog a few steps to catch up with Sophie. I put my hand on her shoulder. She looks up and smiles as I guide her to the bus.

When we walk onto the plane, Gary Randall's staring at Sophie. In my eight years with the organization, he's never flown on the same plane with the team. He has a private jet that I'm sure is much nicer.

"Sophia," he says, patting the seat next to him, "sit with me."

I step in front of her. "You know, Gary, I was hoping to have a chat with you, so this is good timing."

He stares at me as I plop down in the seat across the aisle from him. Sophie walks by and ducks into a seat a couple of rows behind us.

"What have I done to deserve this honor?" Gary says,

staring at me warily. "Seb Miller wants to spend time with me. That's never happened."

"It's happening now," I say, staring back at him. "I understand you hired Sophie to find out who asked for Liza Murray to be kicked out of the clubhouse. I think you already know it was me."

"I didn't know, but I suspected. It's given the team a lot of bad press—even national media. You want to tell me why?"

"No, I don't, but it's not because she's a woman."

"Did you sleep with her?" He lowers his voice. "Is that the reason the paper fired her?"

"I didn't sleep with her, but even if I did, that's none of your business."

"Everything about you became my business when you signed that contract for two hundred million."

"Naw, that contract is for play on the field. It doesn't entitle you to anything else."

"It entitles me to get a return on my investment—hopefully, a very large one. If you're distracted, it affects your play on the field."

I laugh and shake my head. "Have you seen my stat line lately? Does it look like I'm negatively affected by anything?"

"I need you to do a press conference and explain why you asked for Liza to be removed. It's the only way to get past this."

"That's not happening. The story will fade away like they all do."

"It's been almost a month and they're still talking about it." He checks his phone and then looks back at me. "We need to at least tell them it was you."

"Tell them what you want," I say, standing up. He puts his hand on my arm.

"You know, Seb. You work for me. You seem to forget that. How'd you like to be playing in Minnesota by this time next year?"

I lean down so I'm only a few inches from his face. "Home plate looks the same in every stadium, Gary. I don't give a shit where I play."

He laughs. "You better take a closer look at their record before you say that."

"I think we both know if you trade me, their wins are going to go up and yours are going to crash. Do what you want. I'm good either way."

As I walk to the back of the plane, I glance at Sophie who's sitting with Ken. She has a little bit of panic in her eyes. I smile at her. When she smiles back, the panic goes away.

Chapter Twenty-One

SOPHIE

Seb's barely walked past me when I see Gary's beady eyes peering at me from over the top of his seat.

"Sophia, come and sit with me," Gary says.

"Ooo," Ken whispers as I stand up, "you're in trouble now."

As I walk up to Gary's aisle, he motions to the window seat next to him without standing up. There's not a chance in hell I'm crawling over him.

"I can't get by you," I say, not trying to hide the growing disdain in my voice. "Scoot over or stand up so I can get to the seat."

He rolls his eyes and huffs as he stands up. He waves dramatically toward the window seat.

"Did you know Seb was the one who asked for Liza to be removed?" he says as he sits back down.

"Yes."

"For how long? And when were you going to tell me?"

"He told me on the way to New York. I was going to tell you when I had a solution to the problem."

"And have you come up with one yet?"

"Well, he won't say why he did it, so—"

"Really, Sophia?" He shakes his head. "Are you that naive? He slept with her. The paper found out about it and fired her. She threatened to reveal it as the reason she was fired. He asked for her to be kept out of the clubhouse and started paying her off to keep her mouth shut. I'm not sure why I hired you if you can't even figure that out."

"I don't think that's it."

"You don't want to think that because I'm guessing you're his next victim."

"Excuse me?" I press my back against the plane's window. "I'm not anyone's victim, and that's completely inappropriate to say."

"Oh, is this a WSM moment?" He lets out a loud grunt. "I seriously don't know why you're paid as much as you are."

"As I've said before, Gary, if we don't see eye-to-eye, we don't have to continue the contract." I cross my arms and lock my eyes with his. "At this point, it might be the best idea."

"We're a week into this, Sophia." He's spitting the words out. "And I'm damn sure not going to lose money on you. Figure out a way to make this story go away, then you can go away."

"The story will fade out. It's already started. Liza's back in the clubhouse. If Seb won't say why he did it, there's no reason to tell the media it was him. It just starts the news cycle up again." I lower my voice. "But I think the media is making a bigger deal out of this than they normally would because they sense a pattern of inappropriate behavior within the organization as a whole."

He glowers at me but doesn't say anything. I'm not sure he's even breathing right now.

"Do you know of anyone else associated with the team—staff, owners, players—who has exhibited bad behavior?" I hold his stare.

"No," he says through clenched teeth. "Do you?"

"Not yet."

"Because there's nothing to know. I run a tight ship. And I've told you before, I didn't hire you to look into anything else except the Liza Murray incident. Do your damn job and get the media to quit slandering my team." He stands up and waves his hand—dismissing me. "Now go find somewhere else to sit. I'm done talking to you."

Ken looks up at me as I sit down next to him again. "You get fired?"

"No such luck."

He laughs. "Well, if you're trying to get fired, keep hanging out with Seb. That's the best way to get it done. We have a strict no mingle policy between staff and players."

"First, I'm not hanging out with Seb. He's hanging out with me—"

"Doesn't matter. Same outcome. It's up to the staff to spurn player advances."

"Well, that's some bullshit right there. How about we put the blame where it belongs? On the pursuers."

"You're not wrong, but it's still something we make clear

to our staff upfront—no personal mingling of any kind with the players. And that includes the men on the staff. We have to discipline guys all the time for trying to hang out with the players at bars and stuff. Strictly not tolerated."

"Well, I'm not officially staff. I'm a consultant. I'll be out of here in a few weeks tops."

He shuts his laptop and looks at me. "That fast? You think you've come up with the magic solution to get the media to stop talking about Liza?"

"Working on it," I say, lowering my voice. "You were the one who pulled her credentials. Do you want to tell me why?"

"Joe told me she was harassing a player."

"Seb already told me it was him."

Ken jerks his head around to look at me. "I can't believe he told you. He barely told me."

I shrug. "What do you mean by 'harassing'?"

"Making him feel uncomfortable," he says. "That's all I needed to know. My job is to protect the franchise, and that's Seb."

"Uncomfortable how?"

"I don't know. He didn't offer that information and I didn't ask."

"Why'd you reinstate her? Did Gary tell you to?"

He sinks in his seat and whispers, "Gentry told me to first. I ignored him, but then he must have told his daddy because I got called up to Gary's office the next day. He told me to give Liza her credentials back."

"Did you tell him she was harassing Seb?"

"No," he says, looking away from me. "I told Joe I

wouldn't tell anyone. Frankly, I can't believe this story still has legs. I have no idea why it's still around."

"Sure you do," I say. "It's because of the harassment complaints about Gentry. The media senses it's a culture issue."

He sits up straighter. "Did Gary tell you about all that? I'm shocked."

"Nope, but you just did."

"Very sneaky, Sophia," he growls as he sinks back down into the seat.

"I'm not going to tell anyone you confirmed it. The media already knows."

"They suspect. They don't know. I've been doing everything I can to bury it."

"Hmm," I say. "I mean, I know that's your job, but that's not a great thing to keep buried. The team could get a lot of credit for coming clean about it and showing the world how they're trying to improve."

"I know you haven't been here that long, but surely you've figured out how Gary works. He's all about the cover-up and spin, especially where his family's concerned."

"He might be all about that, but I'm certainly not."

"Be careful, Sophia. If you talk negatively about Gentry or any of Gary's family, you're not only going to be fired, Gary's going to ruin your reputation and your business."

I stare at him for a second. "Is that a threat?"

"No," he says, opening his laptop. "It's just a fact. I've seen it happen before. Gary's an asshole."

"If he's such an asshole, why do you prop him up?"

"Because I need this job," he says, shaking his head. "I've

got a wife and two kids to support. No one in this organization has the balls to go against Gary."

I nod as I sink back into my seat. I think it might be time for someone to stand up to Gary, and I'm getting the feeling that I'm the only person willing to do it.

Chapter Twenty-Two

SEB

"Hey, Soph." I jog to catch up with her when we get off the plane. "Are you going back to the stadium? I need a ride."

"What?" She holds her hands over her head as the rain starts coming down harder. "Where's your car?"

"Back at the stadium. I rode over here with Joe." I grab her bag and push her toward her car. "Come on, we're getting wet."

She hesitates, but then starts walking. "Why aren't you riding back there with Joe?"

"Uh, I'm kind of pissed at him right now." She clicks her car open. I open the passenger's side door and reach for her keys. "Get in. I'll drive."

"What? No," she says, pulling her keys away from me. "It's my car. I'll drive."

"I thought you said you were scared of hurricanes."

"It's just rain, Seb." She wipes some raindrops from her forehead. "I'm not scared of rain."

"Yeah, and we're getting soaked by that rain right now. Get in." I grab the keys out of her hand, push her into the car, and close the door.

After I put our luggage in the back, I crawl into the driver's seat and move the seat as far back as it will go. She's staring at me when I look over.

"Seb, do you want to talk about your control issues?" She's nodding her head slowly like she's a therapist.

"What?" I say, laughing. "I don't have control issues."

"I'm a really good driver," she says. "I do it all the time."

"I'm sure you are. This is way more about me than you. I hate being the passenger."

"Control issues."

"Probably." I look over at her and smile. "Is our time up for this session, Dr. Banks?"

"Yes," she says, smiling. "We can dig into this more in our next session. Besides, I kind of like being the passenger—and I rarely am—so if you can figure out how to make your legs fit into that side of the car, I'm fine with you driving."

"Thank you." I start the car up. It sputters a little bit before it engages. "How old is this thing?"

She gasps and throws her hand to her chest. "What? Did you just call Jackson a thing?"

"And Jackson is who? Your car?"

"My Jeep. Jackson Jeep. Show him some respect." She runs her hand lovingly over the dashboard. "Don't look at me like that. It's the perfect name for him. Why? What's your car named?"

"My car doesn't have a name."

She breathes in sharply like I told her something shocking.

"We should give it one right now before it has to suffer through any more of an identity crisis."

I shake my head. "It's not getting a name because it's a car."

"It's a Range Rover, right?" She taps her fingers on her lips and squints like she's trying to solve a difficult math equation. "Ronald? Ronald Range Rover?"

"No."

"Ricky? Randall? Randy?"

I'm staring at her, trying to keep a straight face, but I'm starting to break. She's so damn adorable when she's talking nonsense.

"Ooo!" She throws her hands over her mouth. "Rock!"

I nod. "If my car's going to have a name, it can be called The Rock."

"Rock Range Rover—"

"No," I say, holding up my hand. "It doesn't have a last name. It's just The Rock."

Her face is serious like we're approving a treaty. "Agreed."

I glance in the rearview mirror and see Joe tailing us. He was not happy when I told him I was riding with Sophie, but he kept his mouth shut.

"Is that Joe?" she says, looking back. "Are you mad at him for following us?"

"No, he follows me everywhere. I'm sure you've figured that out by now. The team makes him. He's just doing his job."

"Then why are you mad at him?"

"Why did you tell Roman you had a bad feeling about

him?" I glance at her and then look back at the road. "Did Joe do something to you?"

"No, but he told me to back off of you—to not dig any deeper into why you had Liza removed."

"That's why I'm pissed at him," I say, trying to loosen my death grip on the steering wheel. "He doesn't need to be telling you to do anything."

"He apologized, but I get the feeling he's covering something up."

"For me?" I take another peek at her.

"Maybe," she says slowly, "but I was talking more about covering for Gentry."

"Covering what for him?" My head snaps toward her. "Roman said something about Gentry to me. What's going on? Is he bothering you?"

"I think he bothers everyone." She lets out a tense laugh.

"Yeah, that's for sure, but what aren't you telling me?"

"What aren't you telling me?" She crosses her arms again.

I ignore her last question. "About Gentry, Sophie. What aren't you telling me? What did he do?"

She sighs. "He hasn't done anything—to me."

"Meaning?"

"I don't know. There's a rumor going around that he might have a pattern of harassment against female employees of the team. I don't know for sure. I don't have any solid proof."

I pull over to the side of the road and stop the car. "I want you to stay away from him," I say, taking her hands.

"You sound like Joe now," she says. "Do you know something?"

"I don't know anything. I mean, I know he's an asshole,

but this is the first I'm hearing about that. I don't want you near him anymore."

She stares at me for a second. "Seb, if the rumors are true, he needs to be stopped."

"That's not your job." I squeeze her hands. "Sophie, please don't get near him unless I'm around. Please. I'm worried about you. And I think Roman might kill me if I let anything happen to you. Promise me."

She nods her head. "Okay, I promise. And you're not wrong about Roman."

We both jump as we hear a tap on the window behind me. It's Joe.

"You having car trouble?" he says as I crack the window. He's standing in the pouring rain.

"No, man, sorry. I forgot you were back there. We'll get on the road again."

He nods and heads back to his car.

"Soph, I know you're feeling a little wary of Joe, but I've known him a while. He's a good guy. If I'm not around, you can trust him. Really."

She nods, but I can tell she's not convinced. I put my hand on her leg as I pull back onto the road. She doesn't try to move it. After a minute, she puts her hand on top of mine. I lace my fingers through hers.

"I trust you," she says, smiling at me. A warm feeling shoots all of the way through my body.

"Soph," I say quietly, trying not to scare her. She jumps anyway. "What are you still doing here?"

It's a little before nine. The league finally canceled our game. I didn't think she'd still be in the office, but I found myself wandering up here anyway.

"Oh, hey. You scared me," she says, looking up from her computer. "Did they cancel the game?"

"Yeah, it takes them a while to call it if we haven't played the official five. They hate refunding tickets."

"Is it still raining?" She stretches her arms above her head. She always wiggles her body around when she does that. It's so cute.

"Soph, it's pouring out there. How are you getting home?"

She closes her computer and stands up. "Uh, I'm driving."

"It's been coming down in sheets for like two hours. I'm sure the roads have flooded."

"I'll be careful. I'm fine." She doesn't sound convinced. Her forehead crinkles up as she thinks about what I said.

"You remember that I've driven your car."

"Jackson."

"Yes, I'm sorry. I've driven Jackson. He's not going to be fine in this weather. Will you please follow me to The Rock so I can drive you home?"

"Thank you, but I'm fine." She throws her bag over her shoulder. "I only live fifteen minutes from here."

"Fifteen minutes on a perfect day. You're looking at another hour or so tonight if you're lucky, and that's if your car—"

"Jackson."

149

"Yes, if *Jackson* doesn't drown in a puddle. Soph, it's late. It's crazy outside. I'm driving you home."

"Seb—"

"I'm not trying to get into your place. I know you're not ready for that." She tries to say something, but I hold up my hand to stop her. "No, it's fine. I get it. But no matter how you feel, I care about you. And I want to make sure you're safe tonight. Please let me do that."

"I care about you, too," she says, putting her hand lightly on my chest. "And actually, I would feel better if you drove me home. Thank you."

I smile as I take her hand and lead her out to the parking garage.

"Where's Joe?" she says, looking up at me. "I don't think I've ever seen you without him. Doesn't he follow you home after games?"

"Yeah, he usually follows me home to make sure no one tries to stop my car."

"What do you mean? Like the cops?"

"No, I mean just regular people try to block me in," I say, shrugging, "so they can get an autograph or a picture."

"What? Seriously? Like they try to block your car?"

"The Rock."

"Yes," she says, laughing. "The Rock. Do they try to trap you or something?"

"Yep. It's crazy."

She looks up at me with a new look of concern on her face. "So where is he tonight?"

"There's no way anyone's still out there waiting for players. They would have drowned by now. I sent him home."

"I'm sorry you have to go through stuff like that," she says, touching my arm. "I had no idea it was that bad, Seb."

"Yeah. Most fans are cool, but there are always a few that think you owe them something. They get pretty aggressive and of course, if we get aggressive back, it's a front-page story."

"That's horrible." She smiles up at me as I open her door.

"Welcome to The Rock," I say in my best Sean Connery voice.

"No," she says, putting her hand in my face. "No more of that."

"Yes, ma'am," I say, laughing as I help her into the car. "No puns and no movie quotes. Noted."

It takes us about an hour to drive the five miles to her apartment. Most roads are already closed due to flooding and the others are down to one lane. The rain's still coming down in buckets and the wind's blowing like crazy.

"It's that building," she says, pointing. "The tall one over to the left. Just stop in the middle of the street. I can run from here."

I grab her arm to stop her as she reaches for the door handle. "Soph, it's starting to hail. You're going to get pelted. Hold up. Let me find a place to park."

A huge piece of hail lands on the windshield to accentuate my point.

"Ah!" She wraps her arms around her body. "The Rock is going to get hurt."

"The Rock has very good insurance. I'm more worried about you."

"Go into my parking lot. Turn right after that yellow truck. Do you see the driveway? I have a carport spot."

I follow her instructions until we're parked. The wind's still whipping rain and hail against the car, but at least we're under the carport.

"Do you live close to here?" She grimaces as another gust of wind smashes hail into the side of the car.

"No, I live out in Indian Creek."

"The Bunker? That's like an hour from here on a normal day."

"I'll be fine. Let's just get you into your building safely." I tilt my seat back. "Hold up. I've got a batting helmet back here someplace."

"Do you have another one?" she says as I put it on her head.

"I have a hard skull. No amount of hail is going to penetrate it. Wait for me. I'll come around and get you." I squeeze her shoulder. "We're going to be fine."

The wind tries to take my door off as I open it, but somehow I manage to keep it on its hinges. I make my way around to the passenger's side and hold the door open a crack as Sophie slips out. I pin her to the side of the car as I push the door closed just before another surge of wind whips through. I flatten her against the car with my body.

"I'm going to need to carry you," I yell over the howling wind. "No way you can walk in this."

As I lift her, she wraps her arms and legs around me tightly. "The front door has an awning if you can make it there," she screams. I still can barely hear her.

"All right. Hold on." I wrap my arms around her—one hand holding the helmet firmly on her head—and take off across the parking lot.

I'm over two hundred pounds and the wind's still moving me pretty well. She whimpers directly into my ear as she wraps herself more tightly around me. That jump-starts my adrenaline even further. I think I could run for miles right now.

Chapter Twenty-Three

SOPHIE

"Soph? You okay?"

We've made it into the lobby of my apartment building, but I can't seem to release myself from his body. My arms are wrapped around his neck so tightly that I'm surprised he's not choking.

"Yeah," I say, my voice shaking. "Give me a second, okay?"

"Take all the time you need," he whispers as he strokes my soaking wet hair. I'm not sure what happened to the batting helmet. It must have blown off at some point.

I finally release my death grip on his neck and look at him.

"Are you crying?" he says softly. "Soph, we're safe. I'm not going to let anything happen to you. I promise."

I nod as I wipe the tears off my face. "You'd think after living here for eight years I'd be used to hurricanes."

He lowers me to the ground. "The eye of the hurricane is

well north of us. It's a crazy storm, but you'll be fine. I'll walk you to your door."

"Will you stay here tonight?" I say, squeezing his arm.

"What?" He lifts my chin—his eyes searching for more context.

"I mean, you can't drive home, Seb," I say quickly. "It's too dangerous. Just stay here. I have a guest bedroom."

"I can stay here, but I'm not going to do anything that makes you uncomfortable."

"I think you're the one who's going to be uncomfortable. The guest bedroom has a queen-sized bed. I'm not sure how well you're going to fit on it."

"I'll be fine," he says, putting his arm around me. "Let's get you dried off. You're shivering."

"What? I look good," Seb says as he walks out of the guest room, wearing a sheet like a toga. His clothes are in the dryer.

"I'm not saying you don't." I hold up wine and beer to give him a choice. He points to the beer. "It's definitely your look, but you could wear some of the clothes Sam left over here."

"I'm not wearing that asshole's clothes." He sits at my kitchen counter and takes a long drink of his beer. "And we're getting rid of his clothes tomorrow. Pack them up. I'll burn it for you."

"Or maybe give it to Goodwill."

"They don't take asshole clothes." His eyes aren't blinking. "You still have a thing for him or something?"

"Not even a little bit. I just haven't had time to get rid of his stuff."

"Does he still call you?"

"Not since Maisie shut him down." I laugh into my wine glass. "She showed up at his work and tore him a new one in front of all of his colleagues."

"She's pretty little to be your enforcer."

"She grew up with all brothers—we both did. We had to get tough pretty early in life."

He smiles. "You don't seem too tough to me."

"Don't let my performance from tonight fool you. Hurricanes are about the only things that scare me. And stuff being thrown at me—although not anymore."

"And air turbulence and toothpicks."

"Everyone should be scared of those," I say, smiling at him. "I'm sure you're not scared of anything."

"Uh, I don't love snakes and I'm deathly afraid of dancing."

I choke on my wine as I start laughing. "Dancing?"

"Freshman year homecoming. I stepped on my date's foot and broke her toe."

"What? Oh my God." I'm laughing so hard that my eyes are starting to water. "You broke her toe?"

"Don't make fun of me," he says, pointing at me.

"I'm not. I promise." I press my lips together tightly to try to quit laughing. "Did you have to take her home?"

"Yeah," he says. "She couldn't walk. Her dad was so pissed at me. I haven't danced since. These feet are deadly weapons."

"Well, we might have to work on that at some point."

"I'm not dancing ever. You can't make me." He walks over and stirs the pot that's reheating some leftover pasta sauce. "This smells amazing. Homemade?"

"Yeah, I love cooking when I have time."

"Me, too," he says, looking at me almost shyly. "My mom taught me how. I was kind of a quiet kid. I liked hanging out with her in the kitchen."

"What's your favorite thing to make?" I push myself up until I'm sitting on the counter. He seems to have taken over the cooking.

"I like to grill, but that's not really cooking. I guess holiday meals. You know, when everyone's in the kitchen cooking the whole spread. My specialty's sweet potatoes. I like to make them a little spicy."

I watch him for a second as he multi-tasks between the sauce and the noodles. He's nothing like I expected him to be. "Where do you spend the holidays?"

"Back in Michigan where I grew up. My folks still live there—pretty close to Grand Rapids. You said you'd only been here eight years. I thought you were a native."

"Nope," I say. "Chicago—just around the lake from you. I moved here for college and never left."

"You like it here?"

"I like the weather. Chicago's too cold but it's miserable here in the summer, too. I've always thought if I had enough money, I would seek seventy-degree temperatures all year round."

"What? Like chase that temperature around the globe?" He takes a few noodles out of the pot and tastes them.

"Yeah, like just keep moving all of the time."

"Or you could move to San Diego."

"No, I don't like the Pacific Ocean. It's too cold for me. I want to swim without a wetsuit." I drain my glass of wine. He pours me another. "Do you want a Caprese salad to go with the pasta?"

After he puts our plates of spaghetti on the island, he lifts me off the counter and lets his hands linger around my waist. I take a sharp breath as I look up at him. My body temperature shoots up when I see his intense eyes.

"I don't know what a Caprese salad is," he says as he releases me, "but yeah, I'm sure I'd eat it."

I open the refrigerator to get the salad ingredients and stand there for a second to let the cold air bring my temperature back to normal.

"Okay," he says, taking the tomato and cheese out of my hands and closing the refrigerator. "I have the money to make this seventy-degree thing work. Let's decide where we're headed for the year."

"What?"

"I mean just for fun. Let's decide where we would go."

"Hmm," I say as I cut into the block of mozzarella. "I've always wanted to live in The Keys, but you know, the whole hurricane thing, so maybe we can start there in January after the storms are gone."

"Okay, I like that. It starts getting too hot down there probably in May, so maybe the mountains after that?"

"No, too cold in May. How about we head over to Italy for May and June? Rome, The Amalfi Coast. It's perfect there that time of year."

"Nice. Pasta, wine, we seem to be developing a theme. What's after June?"

He takes the salad plates from me, sets them on the island, and then pulls out my stool. Everything he's doing right now is so intimate. I'm not sure he even notices, but I'm finding it hard to even catch my breath.

"Soph?"

"Oh, yeah," I say, shaking my head. "Then the mountains, like The Rockies or Lake Tahoe."

"You've thought about this."

"Maybe," I say, smiling as I dig into the salad.

"It probably starts snowing in the mountains in October. I don't love snow. Where should we go?"

"Yeah, where's a good place in the fall?"

"Actually, the Midwest is pretty in the fall," he says as he refills my glass again. "Maybe we'll go back and visit our families in the fall."

"I'm not sure I can stay with my family for an entire season."

"My parents have a vacation house on Lake Michigan. We can stay there and take day trips to visit our families. It's beautiful in the fall. That's where I go after the season to unwind a bit."

"Sounds amazing," I say. Like really amazing. Why does it feel like I'm planning my life with him? And why does it feel so perfect? "Then for the holidays, we might want snow."

"Back to the mountains?" He polishes off his spaghetti. I push my half-eaten plate to him. He starts in on it immediately.

"No, maybe like Vermont or something," I say, watching him closely. God, he's beautiful. I've been trying not to notice that, but everything about him—inside and out—is beautiful. "Vermont would be pretty."

"Vermont is really cold in the winter," he says, pointing at me.

"We can snuggle." I try to stop it from coming out of my mouth.

He spits out a little of his beer. "We can?" he says, his eyes wide.

"Oh, wow. I think that's the wine talking. I'm a lightweight."

"I remember." His eyes are intense again. "But just so we're clear, I'd like to snuggle with you. Whenever you're ready."

I want to crawl across the island and throw my body into his. I somehow hold myself back.

"Maybe I should call it a night before I do something stupid again." I slip off the barstool and walk around to put my wine glass in the sink.

"I'll clean up. I'm not tired yet," he says, taking my glass from me. His eyes are searching mine for an invitation. I look down. "Do you need me to tuck you in again?"

"I think I'll be okay," I say, hugging him. "Thank you for taking such good care of me tonight."

"Any time. I mean that. All I want to do is take care of you." As I start to walk away, he puts his hand on my arm. He's smiling when I look up at him—a sweet, gentle smile. "And you've never done or said anything stupid to me—even that first night. You're perfect."

I take a quick breath in and nod. My mind's completely blank. I can't think of a reply that would be even close to adequate.

He squeezes my arm. "Good night, Sophie," he says as he turns around and starts rinsing the dishes.

Chapter Twenty-Four

SEB

I haven't been able to sleep all night. I'd like to blame it on the storm that's still raging outside, but I know it's because Sophie's sleeping fifty feet from me. I can't quit thinking about how I'd like to be holding her tightly right now. As another clap of thunder shakes the windows, I see the bedroom door open a crack.

"Soph?"

She opens the door wider and peeks in. The light in the hallway's backlighting her so I can see her hair flowing down over her shoulders and onto the t-shirt she's wearing. It doesn't look like she's wearing pants.

"Are you okay?"

"Yeah," she whispers.

"The wind's picking up again. It's getting pretty loud."

"Yeah." I can barely hear her.

"Sophie, nothing's going to happen. It's probably just the last bands of the storm. We're safe here."

"Okay." She starts to take a step into the room but then leans against the door frame.

As I turn on the lamp next to my bed, she shifts around a little bit. She's definitely not wearing pants. I see a little bit of her lacy underwear peeking out from underneath her shirt.

"Do you want to sleep in here with me?" I can already see in her eyes that she does, but I'm not going to push her. "I promise I won't touch you."

"What if I want you to touch me?" she says, smiling a little bit as she looks up at me.

"Is that the wine talking?"

"The wine wore off an hour ago."

"Is it the storm talking?" I motion toward the window as another clap of thunder breaks.

"Why can't it just be me talking?"

"It can," I say, scooting over to the side of the bed. "Is it?"

"Yeah. I kind of like you."

"Kind of, huh?" I say, laughing. "Well, that's a start."

"I didn't mean it like that," she says. "I really like you."

"I really like you, too."

She smiles again but doesn't move from the door.

"Come here, Sophie," I say, opening my arms.

She starts to walk over, but when a howling gust of wind shakes the walls, she shrieks and throws herself into me.

"The storm's going to go away, Soph," I whisper into her hair as I wrap my arms around her. "You don't need to be scared."

"The wind sounds like a train's about to crash into the house," she says, rubbing her forehead against my chest. "I remember that from the last time. It's horrifying."

"I promise the apartment isn't going to blow apart." I start rubbing her back. "And we're upstairs, so no flooding. We're safe."

She nods but doesn't say anything. As more thunder explodes, she jumps into my lap and curls into a ball against my chest. I pull her body closer to mine.

"You're okay," I say, kissing the top of her head.

She finally looks up—her soft eyes shining at me. "That's the second time you've kissed me. I know you kissed me that first night—even though you left that part out when you were recapping the story."

I smile. "You know because you remember or because Maisie told you?"

"Maisie."

"Well, it's not a first kiss if you don't remember it, and a kiss on the head doesn't count, so we still haven't officially kissed."

She shifts around so she's straddling my lap.

"Hmm," she says, tilting her head. "I wonder if there's something we can do about that."

"I don't like to kiss women unless they're going to remember it," I say, holding her face between my hands. "How's your memory working tonight?"

"Good—"

She barely gets it out before my lips land on hers. As she circles her arms around my neck, I push her lips open and start exploring with my tongue. She wraps her legs around my waist. I pull her farther into me as she starts grinding up against me.

As I tug on one of her lips with my teeth, she lets out a soft moan. It's more than I can take. I yank her shirt over her head and finally look at the curves I've been dreaming of seeing.

"Damn, Sophie. Your body is unbelievable." As I start exploring her breasts with my hands, she tugs at my shirt.

"Off," she demands. Her bossy, little voice almost makes me cum on the spot.

"Yes, ma'am," I say, pulling the shirt over my head.

"Stop it!" she says, leaning back from me.

"What?" I say, laughing. "I thought you wanted me to take my shirt off."

"Oh my God, Seb." She runs her hands over my chest. "How does anyone have a chest that looks this good?"

I press my chest against hers as I start exploring her neck with my tongue. She wiggles around on my lap. Her back's arching hard, pushing her chest against mine. Just having her body smashed against me feels so good. I can't imagine how good it's going to feel to be inside her. She grinds into me again. I'm hard as a rock underneath her. She reaches down and rubs me a few times through my boxers. It takes all of my concentration not to explode.

I flip her onto her back and flatten her underneath me. She wraps her legs around me as my tongue plunges deep into her mouth again. When her hips start bucking against me, I reach down and try to pull off her underwear. My body's still pressed against her. I don't want to move, so I rip the underwear off with one hard tug. As they tear away, she lets out a gasp mixed with a little giggle. God, the sex sounds she makes are going to be the end of me.

"I would have taken them off," she whispers into my ear. She gives my earlobe a little tug with her teeth.

"No time for that," I growl. "Things to do."

She giggles again underneath me.

"Sophie," I moan as I hump her. Her body starts moving with mine.

As my hand starts crawling down her body, she shudders and lets out a little whimper.

"Just hold on, baby," I whisper. "It's going to be a good night."

Chapter Twenty-Five

SOPHIE

The minute he rips my panties off, my body starts writhing uncontrollably underneath him. My hips buck up and down like I'm riding a bull. I've pretty much lost all control. At this point, all I can do is hold on for dear life.

"Sophie," he moans as his lips crash back down onto mine.

He's on top of me, flattening me beneath him. My body's tingling so hard. I think I'm going to cum just from the feeling of his beautiful chest against mine. Why does his chest look like it was carved by Michelangelo? Good God, I knew it was going to be good, but—

"Ahh." My mind engages again as his hand starts sliding down my body. He sticks a few fingers inside me and then starts rubbing with his thumb. My body jolts when he hits the spot.

"You good?" he whispers thickly against my neck where his mouth continues to explore—licking, sucking, biting.

"Yeah." I barely get it out when my body starts shaking.

He has me between his thumb and finger, rubbing faster. He puts one of his other fingers back inside me and starts pumping it in and out. God, he's good with his hands. And fast, holy crap, I think I'm going to cum already.

"Ahhh," I groan as my body shudders against him.

"That's good, baby." He's looking right into my eyes— watching me fall apart. "Don't hold back. Let it all out."

After my body stops vibrating, I collapse into a puddle below him. He kisses me a few times, smiling as he lifts his head to give me time to catch my breath.

"Oh my God." I manage to get out. "I think I'm having an out-of-body experience. Am I still on the bed?"

He rolls off me and pulls me onto his chest. He rubs my back a few times. "It feels like your body's still here," he says, laughing.

"Just barely." I climb on top of him and straddle his chest. "You know what you're doing."

"I just respond to the feedback I'm getting," he says, grabbing my butt with both his hands, "and you were giving me some really good feedback."

His eyes turn hungry again when I grind my butt into his hands. He squeezes it one more time and then reaches for my breasts. I push his hands back down. "Not yet. You still have a piece of clothing on."

He reaches for me again. I swat his hands away.

I tug at his boxers. "I seem to remember somewhere back in that orgasm haze that you ripped my panties off."

"Yeah, sorry about that. I'll buy you a new pair." He's blushing a little bit. Good God. Could he get any sexier? "Or you can rip mine off."

"I'm not sure you've left me that kind of strength."

He lifts his hips and starts pulling his boxers off. As I rise to my knees to give him a little space, he starts sucking urgently on one of my breasts. Would it be wrong if I came again so soon?

He pushes me back down. As I sit up, I feel the tip of him against my butt. I reach back and take him in my hand—big and hard as a rock.

"Do you have a condom?"

"Yeah," he says, "but I'm clean. We get tested at the start of every season and I always use a condom."

"But you don't want to now?" I'm still rubbing him with my hand.

"I'll do anything you want," he says, closing his eyes as I run my fingers over the tip. "But yeah, I want to be inside you without a condom."

"I got tested after I found out that Sam cheated on me. I'm clean, too."

He opens his eyes. "You didn't have to tell me. I trust you."

"I thought you said you had trust issues, too."

"Not with you." He pulls me down on top of him and kisses me gently before he growls, "I want to be with you and only you for as long as you'll have me. I won't cheat on you. I'm clean, but you're calling the shots here."

For some reason, I trust him. I don't know why. It's not like me at all. The trust surges through me like a bolt of electricity. I grab his face and kiss him. He laces his fingers through my hair and pulls my lips harder against his.

I finally break away and look at him once before I start

licking my way down his body. His fingers are running through my hair as I keep sinking lower. When I lick the tip, he shudders a little bit. Good, it's his time to fall apart.

He grabs my hair as I lick and kiss and inhale. After a few minutes, his hips start to shake. He's not going to be able to hold on much longer. Just when I think I'm about to finish him, he sits up and reaches under my arms so I'm straddling him again. He lifts my butt with one hand and pushes himself into me with the other. His hands grab my hips and start moving me forcefully on top of him.

He pulls me farther into him as I wrap my legs around his waist. The way he's panting on my neck right now. Good Lord. I think I'm about to pass out. When his shoulders start shaking, it's too much for me. My body starts vibrating with him. I wrap my arms around his neck and hold on. As he explodes inside of me with a loud groan, my body shimmies hard against him. I let out a few whimpers before I collapse on his chest.

"Fuck," he says, panting. "Are you okay?"

"Can't talk." I have to pause. "Right now."

He nuzzles his face into my hair. He's panting so hard that he's blowing the hair off my shoulders.

"My body feels like I just ran a marathon," he says, letting out a long breath.

"Yes, so much that." My chin's resting on his shoulder. I don't think I can lift my head. "I can't move."

He lowers me down onto my back and runs his hand over my stomach. "I think we both could use some water before we continue. I'll get it."

"Good because I seriously don't think I could walk right now."

He gives me a soft kiss before he stands up. "Then I think we should make a pact that when I get back with the water, we don't leave this bed until morning."

"Deal."

He crawls out of bed and peeks out the window. "Hey, I think the storm might be over."

"What storm, Seb?" I manage to get out. "What storm?"

Chapter Twenty-Six

SEB

I wake up alone in bed. For a second, I think I might have dreamed the entire night, but I can still smell her sweet scent on the pillows. I glance at my phone. It's four in the morning.

"Soph?" I say, jumping up and heading out into the hallway.

There's a light on in the kitchen. As I turn the corner, I see her sitting on the counter, staring straight ahead.

"Sophie?"

She jumps and then smiles when she sees me. "Hey."

"Hey. Are you okay? It's only four. Why are you up so early?" I push her legs apart as I lean her back up against the cabinets. She wraps her legs around me as I pull her in for a kiss.

"I couldn't sleep." She lays her head against my chest. "I didn't want to wake you up."

"What's wrong?" I start stroking her hair. "Why couldn't you sleep?"

She lets out a long sigh. "I don't know. I have a lot on my mind."

"Why don't you tell me about it? I'm a good listener."

"I'm know you are," she says, smiling as she looks up at me, "but I don't want to talk about it right now. I've got to figure it all out first."

"Baby, I can help you figure it out. I thought you trusted me."

"I do," she says. "I'm not even sure why. It's not like me at all to trust someone this quickly, but I feel safe with you."

"That makes me so happy, baby." I kiss her again. "You can tell me anything."

"I know. Thank you for that." She brushes her hand over my cheek. "But I don't want to talk about it and I'm getting kind of tired again. Can we go back to bed?"

I slide my hands under her butt and lift her. "Yes, I'll carry you. I know how much effort you exerted last night."

She laughs as she wraps her arms around my neck and lays her head on my shoulder. "I think you put in as much effort as I did—if not more."

"God, you're so cute," I say, hugging her to me. "You're so easy to be with."

"So are you." She runs her fingers through my hair. "I've wanted to do that since the first second I saw you. Your hair is beautiful."

I lay her back down on the bed and crawl in beside her. "I thought you didn't remember anything from that night? Except for my eyes."

"Pre-tequila," she says, running her hands through my hair again. "I remember a few things including this beautiful hair."

"I didn't think you noticed me pre-tequila," I say, pulling her onto my chest. "I remember looking at you when I walked into the restaurant. You rolled your eyes at me. It turned me on so much."

"You're turned on by weird things," she says, snuggling into me. "And I definitely looked at you before you even saw me."

"Really? I thought you said you didn't know who I was."

"I had no idea who you were, but I still looked at you." She nuzzles even closer to me. "I mean, come on, Seb, you're beautiful."

"I don't know about that, but if you were interested in me, why'd you roll your eyes?"

"Because I thought you'd be a total asshole. Honestly, I still can't believe you're not." She looks up at me. "I didn't expect this guy at all. You're so sweet."

"I'm sweet to people I care about," I say, brushing her hair out of her eyes. "And I care about you so much. I don't know what it is about you, but God, I'm falling hard for you. Does that freak you out?"

"No," she whispers as she lays her head back down on my chest, "it doesn't freak me out, but you already know, I'm just getting out of a bad relationship. I think I'm a little tentative to get back into something serious. I already had trust issues, and after what happened, they've gotten worse."

"I know, baby," I say, wrapping my arms around her tightly. "I will never lie to you or do anything to hurt you. I promise. Do you believe me?"

"Yeah." She pauses for a second. "I mean, I don't have any

reason not to believe you. It's just going to take some time for me to be fully in, you know?"

"You take all the time you need."

"I think maybe after I'm done working for the team, I'll feel a little bit better about pursuing something with you." She looks up at me again. "I mean if that's what you want."

I lift her chin and lock my eyes with hers. "That's what I want. I don't play games in personal relationships. If you ever want to know where I stand, just ask me. One hundred percent, I want to be in a relationship with you—a committed relationship."

She nods, her eyes getting wider.

"I'm not trying to pressure you," I say, stroking her cheek. "Really, I'm not. Take all the time you need. I just want you to know where I stand. I haven't felt this way in a while, and I've never felt this way so fast. Not even close. I like you—every single thing about you."

She smiles. "You didn't really like my catching phobia. You were kind of grumpy about it."

"I'm a catcher, Sophie. I can't have my friends, much less my girlfriend, not knowing how to catch."

"Girlfriend?"

"Yeah, I mean that's what I want," I say. "It's okay if you're not there yet."

"I'm not there yet," she says. "I like you so much, but I need to take it more slowly. Are you sure you're okay with that?"

"I'm absolutely fine with that. No pressure. Okay?"

She nods. "Okay. I trust you. I think. It feels weird, but I think I might."

"I will never give you a reason not to trust me. Never. I promise." I roll her over and spoon her to me. "Do you think you can sleep now?"

She wiggles back against me. "Yeah, I think I can. I like when you're wrapped around me like this. I feel safe."

"You are safe, baby. You're always safe with me. I'll never hurt you or let anything else hurt you. I promise."

Chapter Twenty-Seven

SOPHIE

After Seb carried me back to bed last night, I didn't wake up once. Having his body wrapped around me felt so safe and comfortable.

When I finally wake up, I find him nibbling on my neck. His soft curls are rubbing against my face.

"Excuse me. I was sleeping," I say, running my fingers through his hair.

"Hmm." He licks his way up my face until he lands on my lips. "Time to wake up."

As he starts kissing me, I run my hands over his chest. Sadly, there seems to be a shirt over it.

"Wait," I say, sitting up and wrapping the blankets around me, "why are you dressed?"

"I have to leave." He tries to tug the blankets down. "We have a day game today."

"No," I say, holding them around me. "Either get naked or you can't access what's underneath here."

"Are you sure?" He smiles as his hand runs over the blankets down my body. "I have a few minutes and my mouth kind of wants to be down here again."

"A few minutes?" I swat at his hand. "It's going to take longer than that."

"Really?" He raises his eyebrows—his eyes twinkling underneath them. "It didn't last night."

"Wow." I feel myself blushing a little bit. "Someone's a little full of himself this morning."

"I'm just saying." He growls as he kisses me again. "I want to stay and hear all those sexy little sounds you make—God, I want to—but I have to go. I need to run by my house before I head to the stadium."

"What time is it?" As I yawn, I stretch my arms up causing the blankets to fall.

He dives into me—burying his face between my breasts.

"Seven," he mumbles. "Is it possible to stay right here for the rest of the day?"

"I wish." I rub my face into his hair.

"Grrr!" He sits up and shakes his head. "I hate being an adult. I have to go. I'll have one of the security guys swing by to take you to your car when you're ready."

"No, It's fine. I'll call an Uber."

"That's not safe," he says, running his hands over my shoulders. "Let me send someone."

"Do you know how many cars, cabs, planes, and trains I've taken successfully without your help?"

He smiles. "You didn't know me then. Now that you do, let me help you."

"You can help me with certain things, Mr. Control Issues,

but I can get to the stadium by myself."

"Okay, okay." He brushes his hand over my cheek as he comes in for another kiss. "Will you at least find me when you get in? I'll worry whether you want me to or not. And I was thinking maybe tonight I could cook for you at my place after the game. Unless you want to go out to a restaurant—"

"Seb," I say, grabbing his arm, "I'm still working for the team. We can't be seen together in a personal setting."

He's kissing my neck again. It's making me want to rip off his clothes with my teeth.

"We'll go to my place then," he whispers. "The only person who will know is Joe."

"Joe works for the team." I rub my face against his cheek. I like the way his stubble feels. I like the way everything about him feels. "This can't happen again until I'm done with this assignment. It probably shouldn't have happened last night, but I'm glad it did."

He scoots back from me. "So, what? This was like a one-night stand or something?"

"What? You know it wasn't. I wanted this to happen. I want it to happen again, but I need to finish this contract first."

He nods, but his face is starting to tighten. "When are you done?"

"I'm not sure." I'm finding it hard to hold his stare. His eyes have gotten so intense.

"What do you still have to do?" His voice drops into a low growl. "You know I'm the one who asked for Liza to be removed. That's why they hired you. Do you want me to call Ray Franklin and tell him? Then it can be out in the media and you can stop working for the team."

"No, don't do that. The story's fading out. Let it die."

"Good, then you're done." He scoots closer to me again and tilts my chin up to look at him. "Unless you're doing something else. Tell me what it is."

"I can't tell you. I signed a non-disclosure."

"Seriously? After everything we said—and did—last night? You can trust me. You know that. I'm not going to tell anyone." He gets right in my face. "Sophie, it better not have anything to do with Gentry."

"I'm fine. I can tell you this much. I think the first story about Liza being banned was just the tip of the iceberg."

"Meaning?"

"Meaning, I think there's a culture of bad behavior in the front offices and I think the media senses it. I want to get at that before I'm done."

He walks over to the window and draws the curtains back. Sunshine comes streaming in. "I mean, yeah, that's important," he says, turning back toward me, "but I don't know how safe it is for you. I don't like it."

"I'll be fine. Trust me." I grab my robe off of the floor. "And speaking of trust, are you ready to tell me why you asked for Liza to be removed from the clubhouse?"

He looks out the window for a few more minutes, then finally turns around. His eyes look sad. "I can't tell you, Soph. Will you trust me that it was for a good reason?"

"Gary thinks she slept with you and that it's the reason she got fired. I've already asked you, but did you sleep with her?"

He walks swiftly across the room and puts his hands on my shoulders. "No, Soph. No. I told you. Of course not. But are you asking me that personally or professionally?"

"I don't know." I shrug. "Maybe both."

His phone beeps. As he digs it out of his bag, I head to the kitchen to get some coffee.

"It's Joe. He's freaking out because he doesn't know where I am."

"Don't tell him you're here. Seriously, Seb. I don't want anyone to know."

His eyes narrow. "Again, are you saying that personally or professionally?"

"Professionally." I hand him a cup of coffee. "When I'm done with the team, I don't care who knows about us."

He takes a deep breath and walks over to me, taking my hand into his. "Look, Soph, I have to leave. Can we talk about this after the game?"

"Yeah," I say as he kisses me on the forehead. "Of course."

"Okay. Call me when you get to the stadium."

"Unless my driver kidnaps me or something."

"So not funny, Sophie." He points at me as he closes my front door. "Lock the door behind me."

I walk over and click the deadbolt.

"Thank you." I hear from the other side of the door.

I lean against it and whisper through the door crack. "Go, you weirdo. You're going to be so late. They're going to fine you."

"Worth every penny," he whispers as he smacks a kiss through the door.

Chapter Twenty-Eight

SEB

"Seb!" When I walk out of Sophie's building, one of her neighbors takes my picture as I'm going to the car. "Hey, can I get a shot with you?"

He jogs over and tries to get me to pose for a selfie. I don't. I do my best to ignore him as I pull some palm branches off the hood of my car. I slide in and lock the doors. I have my windows blacked out, so he can't take another picture, but that's not stopping him from trying.

"C'mon, Seb, it will only take a second." He bangs on the windows.

My phone rings. It's Joe again.

"Hey," I say, starting my car up. I rev the engine extra loud to try to get the fan to back off.

"Where the fuck are you? I'm at your place. The gate security guard said you didn't come home last night."

"Yeah, I stayed at a hotel." As I back out, the fan flips me off. "I didn't want to make the drive in that storm. It was crazy. I'm headed home now."

"From where?" he growls. "You know it's a day game today, right?"

"Yeah, man. I'll be there in a bit. I'm over by Coconut Grove."

I hear him let out a deep breath. "That's like an hour from here. You're going to be late. Bud will lose his mind."

"He's going to have to deal with it. He can fine me if he wants."

"Hold up," he says. "I'm getting a media alert on you. You didn't kill anybody last night, did you?"

I don't answer. My mind's still back with Sophie. I'm not sure I'm going to be able to think about anything else today.

"Hotel, huh? Some guy posted a picture of you leaving an apartment complex. He says you were a douche and wouldn't pose for a selfie with him."

"Yeah, well, he's not wrong about that."

"Whose apartment? Were you with Sophie last night?"

I don't say anything.

"Seb, we talked about that."

I pause for a second. "Look man, I don't know what happened between you and her, but I like her. I want to date her. If you're going to keep working with me, you need to get on board. Bottom line."

"She told Gary you were the one who got Liza kicked out—"

"I told Gary."

"Seb—"

183

"What's he going to do about it?" I yell. "Fire me? I've got a five-year guaranteed contract."

He blows out a breath again. He does that a lot when he's trying not to tell me to fuck off. "Did you tell him why you did it?"

"It's none of his business, but I don't care anymore, Joe. He can trade me. Whatever. All I'm concentrating on now is Sophie. And trying to get the team into the playoffs."

"And which one is your priority?"

"You know I'm always locked in when I walk onto the field, but there's nothing wrong with having another priority. It's been way too long since I've put energy into my personal life. And it feels nice to finally have someone who's worth the energy."

He doesn't say anything for a second, but finally sighs and says, "Okay, Seb. I'm with you. I've always got your back. You know that."

"I do, but if you want to have my back, have Sophie's back, too." I pause for a second. "I need you to understand that. If we're going to keep working together, she's part of the equation. It's not negotiable anymore."

He doesn't say anything for a full minute, but then finally says, "Yeah, I've got it. If that's what you want, I'll protect her like I protect you. Just get your ass back to the house as fast as you can, so I can get you to the stadium."

As I hang up with him, a text comes through. I glance at it. It's a picture from Sophie. I can't quite make out what it is. I look at it closer to see that it's her underwear—ripped completely apart at the seams.

I laugh as I text back.

Our first official date should probably be at an underwear store or something. You're going to need a lot of replacements. Or maybe quit wearing them all together?

She texts back a smiley face. Yeah, that's the right emoji. I can't quit smiling this morning. I'm not sure I'm going to be able to quit any time soon. I've never felt this happy in a relationship—not even close. I can't believe I just met her. It feels like I've known her for years.

As I get out of my car in the stadium parking garage, some guy I've never seen comes walking over to me.

"Hey, Seb." He's wearing a team badge around his neck, so he must work for the organization. "It's all over Twitter that you spent the night at some apartment complex in Coconut Grove last night. I thought you lived over in the Bunker. Did you have a booty call last night?"

"What the fuck?" I grab him and slam him against a car.

"No!" Joe wedges his way in between us. "You're already late, Seb, and this isn't worth it. Keep walking."

"Man, I didn't mean anything by it." The guy starts following us into the office. "You know, get some where you can."

I whip back around and charge at him again. Joe lowers his shoulder and throws a block into my body.

"Seb, walk!" Joe turns around to the guy and puts his hand up. "You'd be better off to wait a second before you come in. I'm not stopping him next time you say something stupid."

"What the fuck, Joe?" I say as he ushers me through the office door. "I don't know that guy. Why does he feel like he can say something like that? It's bullshit."

"I'll talk to Gary about it. Okay?" Joe keeps pushing me toward the elevators. "I think we should get you a parking spot by the clubhouse so you don't have to walk through here anymore. Probably the best thing for everyone. Now, can we please get on the field before Bud loses his fucking mind?"

"No one is going to talk about her like that," I say, punching the field-level elevator button.

"He doesn't even know who he's talking about. Settle down." He looks at me over the top of his sunglasses. "I've never seen you like this about anyone. Not even your family."

I take a deep breath. "She's special, man. Something about her. I've known it from the first second I saw her."

When the elevator doors open, Gentry and Liza are standing against a wall like they're waiting for someone. They stare at me and start whispering as I walk off.

"What's that about?" I say to Joe as we walk into the clubhouse.

"I have no idea, but with those two, it's never a good thing."

Bud flies over to me when he sees me walk in. "You're ten minutes late for warm-ups. Get your ass on the field. And I'm about to fine you into oblivion."

"Yep, fair enough," I say, heading toward my locker. "Do what you have to do."

Chapter Twenty-Nine

SOPHIE

When I get to the stadium, the first thing I do is text Seb.

Just got to the office.

He texts back immediately.

Thanks for texting. I was getting worried. I just got done with warm-ups. I have a few minutes. Do you want to come down here and entertain me?

A few minutes??? I thought we talked about that. From what I saw last night, I think you can do better.

You're right. I want to take my time with you.
Are you sure we can't see each other tonight?

My text pings again. The smile leaves my face immediately when I see the text is from Gentry.

Sophia, please come and see me when you get in. It's urgent.
I'm working out of my baseball operations office today.

I'm a little leery about meeting with him, but I want to uncover more information on the rumors about him. He's not all that bright. Maybe if I meet with him alone, he'll reveal some information to me. And if he tries something, I know I can take him down. He's not all that strong either.

I text Seb back to tell him we can talk after the game and then head down to Gentry's office. When I walk in, Liza Murray's standing by his desk. They're both smiling at me with their eyes narrow. They look like evil villains about to hatch a dastardly plot.

"What's up?" I say, making sure to stay near the open office door.

"Have a seat, Sophia." Gentry waves to the chairs in front of his desk.

"I'm good," I say, crossing my arms. "I have some work to do before the game. What can I help you with?"

"I think we can help you," Liza says, grabbing a stack of papers off the desk and offering them to me.

I hesitate. I'm sure I don't want to see anything that these two have to offer, but my curiosity gets the best of me. I start leafing through them. They look like her bank statements.

"What am I supposed to be seeing here?" I say, looking up at them. Their faces are eager.

Liza takes the statements back and points at a line item on the first page. It's an automatic deposit for five thousand dollars. I look more closely to see it's from Sebastian Miller. I stop breathing for a second.

"Okay," I say, trying to keep my voice steady. "Seb paid you five grand. For what?"

She sorts through the papers—pointing at the different months at the top of each page and a matching deposit from Seb.

"He pays me five thousand every month," she says, looking from the statements up to me. Her eyes are filled with pity. That pisses me off.

"Why?" She takes a step back when she hears the sharp tone in my voice.

"Why do you think?" She looks at Gentry as she lays the statements on his desk. He's nodding at her—encouraging her to go on. "I slept with Seb. When the newspaper found out, they fired me for sleeping with a player that I was covering. I threatened to tell everyone that it was the reason I was fired. Seb didn't want it to get out, so he started paying me. I'm not proud of it, but when the paper fired me, I didn't have any money saved. I panicked. Seb offered to help me out. I know he only did it to shut me up, but I needed the money."

My head starts spinning. I feel like I'm going to faint. I try to keep my voice even. "Was the sex consensual?"

"Oh yeah," she says, smiling. My hands curl into fists. I want to punch the smile off her face. "It was consensual. Very consensual."

I concentrate hard to keep the anger building up inside me from coming out in my voice. It doesn't work. "So, two consenting adults have sex. You blackmail Seb into paying you to keep quiet about it. He does it. Then he asks for you to be removed from the clubhouse because it's uncomfortable for him to be around you. Am I getting everything?"

"You don't have to get so defensive." Liza laughs as she walks out of the office. "I'm not interested in him anymore. Believe me. He's all yours, but don't say I didn't warn you when he dumps you, too."

I watch her walk out of the office. I can't move. I think I'm in shock. I can't believe he lied to me. I jump when I hear Gentry's voice right behind me.

"Sophia," Gentry says, putting his hand on my shoulder. "It's all over social media that Seb stayed at an apartment complex in Coconut Grove last night. I know that's where you live. I'm guessing that's not a coincidence."

I shove his hand off my shoulder and take a quick step back toward the door. "How do you know where I live?"

"That's not the important thing here." He walks toward me. "I believe it's in your contract that you can't have a personal relationship with any of the players. I'm going to have to tell my dad about it."

"Tell him what you want. My personal life is none of his business, and it's definitely none of yours."

"I don't have to tell him." He takes another step toward me. "Maybe we can make an arrangement."

"I'm not interested in any kind of arrangement with you," I say, spitting the words out. "I'm sure you've tried to make *arrangements* with some other women in this office. Is that what daddy's covering up for you?"

He smiles, trying to mask the surprise in his eyes. "I think you misunderstood me, Sophia. And I'm not sure what you're talking about. Covering up? I think you've been doing this job too long. You're getting suspicious. I was just hoping that you would do a little work for me—personal work."

"Hard pass," I say, turning toward the door. "I'm not doing anything for you."

The minute I turn my back on him, I know it's a mistake. I feel one of his hands on my shoulder, pulling me back toward him, and the other one grabbing my butt.

I put an elbow hard into his eye. He screams as his hands fly over his face.

"If you ever touch me again, you're going to lose a fucking arm," I say, shoving his shoulder.

He looks up, a smile trying to form through his grimaced face. Before he can recover, I kick him hard in the crotch. He grunts and falls to his knees.

"Over the line, Gentry," I say, pointing at him as I back toward the door. "Way over the line."

I keep my eyes on him as I back out of the room. When I'm almost to the door, I run smack into someone else.

"What's over the line?" I hear Seb say from behind me.

Chapter Thirty

SEB

I'm hanging out in the clubhouse, waiting for the game to start, when I see Joe power walking toward me. He looks anxious. I've never seen him look anxious about anything.

"Seb." He looks over his shoulder to make sure no one's listening to us.

"What?" I say as he pulls me over to a corner. "What's wrong?"

"I just walked by Gentry's office."

"Yeah, so."

He hesitates. "I saw Sophie go into his office a few minutes ago."

"What?" My body tenses up. "Alone?"

"Liza Murray walked out a few minutes after Sophie walked in," he says, lowering his voice. "I'm not sure who else is in there. Do you want me to go check?"

"No," I say, throwing my water bottle against the wall. "I've got this."

"Seb." He grabs at my shoulder, but I'm already running down the hallway.

As I bust into Gentry's office, Sophie's backing away from him. He's doubled over on the floor—grabbing his balls.

"Over the line, Gentry," she says, pointing at him. "Way over the line!"

She's backing up and doesn't see us. She crashes into me as I walk toward her.

"What's over the line?" I growl as I circle my arms tightly around her.

She tries to break free of my grip as she looks up at me. Her eyes are wild.

"Get your hands off of me!" She pushes me hard on the chest. When I see the tears in her eyes, I drop my arms and back up a step.

"Baby, what's wrong?" I try to touch her shoulder, but she pulls it away.

"Baby?" Gentry says, looking up. "Well, that's something Dad needs to hear about."

I turn my attention back to Gentry. "Did you touch her?"

Joe wraps his arms around my chest as I start walking toward Gentry. "Seb, we can't do this right now. You have a game to play. You need to be back on the field in ten minutes."

He's pinning my arms to my side, but he knows he can't hold me. He's trying to ease me back. "Seb, come on now. We can finish this later."

"If you touched her, I'm going to fucking kill you."

Gentry scoots into the corner. "Seb, I would never touch Sophia."

I point at him as I charge toward him again. "Don't you fucking say her name."

Joe jumps in front of me and pushes me back again. "Leave this office. Now. We can come back after the game. I promise."

I glare at Gentry one more time before I turn around. Sophie's standing with her back against the wall. Her eyes are still wild. She sees me look at her, spins, and starts running out of the room.

"Sophie!" I bust out of Joe's hold and jog after her. The hallway's filling up with people—owners, media, staff. They're all looking at me.

Sophie turns around slowly as I close in on her.

"Not now, Seb," she whispers. Her voice is shaking. She's trying to keep her face light, but I can tell her eyes are about to release all the tears that are building up. "I don't want to talk about it. Not here."

"Did he hurt you?" I whisper, trying to act as casual as possible. It's taking every bit of restraint in my body not to hug her right now.

"No, *he* didn't hurt me." She's glaring at me now. One tear escapes her right eye and makes its way down her cheek. I want to wipe it off, but I resist.

"What does that mean?" I take a step closer to her. "Soph? What did he say?"

"Seb, you playing tonight?" Bud yells from the clubhouse door. "Or did you take the night off without telling me?"

"Later," Sophie says, turning away from me. "Do not follow me right now."

"Soph." I reach my arm out to her as Joe moves in front

of me.

"Let her go." His eyes are burning a hole through me. He knows I'm about five seconds from being splashed all over social media again and dragging Sophie there with me. "We'll deal with it later. You need to get geared up if you're playing tonight. Seb, you asked me to have her back, too. Following her right now would be the worst thing—for her. You know that."

My eyes are still on Sophie as she walks way too briskly down the hall. "Get somebody on her. Make sure she's safe. I want a report by the middle of the first or I'm walking out of this fucking stadium. I don't care how much it costs me."

"I'm on it," he says as he turns me toward the clubhouse.

The top of the first took almost thirty minutes. Manny's slider is hanging. He gets super slow when that happens. Just what I don't need tonight. Joe's in the dugout when I come off the field.

"Report." I yank off my mask and throw it to our equipment guy.

"She left. I had Max follow her. She's home. That friend from the night we met her just arrived."

"Is she okay?"

"I don't know, Seb. Max said she's really upset." He leans against the wall next to me and whispers. "I snuck into Gentry's office when he left. He had Liza's bank statements on his desk. They show your payments to her. I told you we should have done it from an anonymous account."

A wave of panic shoots through my body. "I've got to get out of here and explain to her."

"You can't leave, man. You know that." He points toward the field. Alex just got on base. That means I'll have to bat this inning. I snap off my chest protector. "Give her some space. We'll deal with it after the game. She's safe."

"Bring me my phone," I say as I grab my batting helmet. "I need to text her."

"And say what? You can't tell her the truth."

"Bring me the phone. I can explain without telling her. She trusts me."

"Does she? That shove to your chest back in Gentry's office would suggest otherwise."

"Bring me my phone."

"You're going to get fined for having a phone in the dugout," Joe says. "This is starting to be an expensive day for you."

"It's well worth any amount of money. I've got to at least try to explain."

As I walk onto the field, I glance back at Manny. "Hey, I need you to keep it tight tonight."

He laughs. "Why? You got someplace worthwhile to go after the game for once?"

I glare at him. "No more throws to first when somebody gets on. Just pitch the damn ball."

"All right, Seb. Just call for my heater all night and we'll be out of here in a tight two."

Chapter Thirty-One

SOPHIE

When I leave Seb, I grab my stuff out of the office and head toward my car. Gary sees me leaving and follows me.

"I just got off the phone with Gentry." He's jogging to try to keep up with me. "He tells me you're sleeping with Seb."

"I'm resigning your account," I say, not turning around. "Effective immediately."

"I don't accept your resignation." He grabs my arm. "If you leave without delivering what you agreed to, I'll sue you and I'll ruin your reputation. You'll never get another job in Miami—or anywhere else."

I jerk my arm away from him and take a quick step toward him. "Don't touch me," I say, glaring down at him. He takes a step back.

"Hey, boss." I look over Gary's shoulder to see Max, Joe's second-in-command on the security team, closing in on us. "Anything wrong?"

"Yes, Max. There is," Gary says, pointing at me. "Ms.

Banks has been fired. She's no longer welcome on our premises. Please take her security badge and follow her out of this garage."

"No problem," Max says. "You should probably go back inside, Mr. Randall. I'll take care of this."

Gary glares at me one more time before he turns back to the offices. I rip my security badge off my shirt and throw it at Max. "You don't need to follow me. I'm leaving."

"I'm following you but not for that asshole," he says as he walks with me to my car. "Joe asked me to make sure you got home okay."

"Do what you want."

As I get in the car, I take a deep breath to try to settle down. All it does is cause the tears that I've held back until now to start streaming down my face. I grab my phone. There are four texts from Seb. I ignore them.

"Soph!" Maisie answers on the first ring. "Where are you? I called you like twelve times last night to see if you were okay. I know the hurricane went wide of us, but the wind was still so scary. Do you remember when we huddled together in our first little apartment all night when Irma came through? I've never been so scared. Sophie? Are you still there?"

"Yeah." It's all I can get out before I start sobbing.

"Sophie! What's wrong? Where are you?" Maisie's yelling, but I can barely hear her over my stuttered breathing. I feel like I'm hyperventilating. "What's happening right now? Sophie!"

"S-s-s-eb," I say, taking a long, shaky breath, "lied to me."

"Seb? Where are you right now? At the stadium?"

"Meet me," I say, sniffing loudly, "at my apartment."

"Sophie, where are you?" Her voice drops into a soothing tone. "Honey, I'll come and get you. You shouldn't drive like this."

"Max is following me home," I whisper.

"Who the hell is Max?" She's yelling again. "Sophia! What's happening right now? I'm calling Roman."

"Don't call Roman!" I wipe the tears off my face. "I'll be home in fifteen minutes. I can't talk anymore right now. Okay?"

"Okay, Soph. I'm leaving my house. I'll be waiting for you." I hear her keys jingling in the background. "Don't hang up, okay? You don't have to talk but don't hang up."

"Okay," I say as I shake my head to try to focus. The tears are still running down my face.

As I leave the garage, I glance in the rearview mirror and see Max pull out behind me. I know I should probably be mad about that, but I'm glad he's following me. I feel like I'm going to pass out. He stays right behind me all the way home.

When I pull into my lot, Maisie's already standing by my parking spot—her phone glued to her ear. I barely get the car parked when she starts tugging at my door.

"Sophie," she says, as she pulls me up into a hug. "What's wrong? I was so worried about you. Just tell me, please."

"Seb lied to me," I say as the tears start to fall harder again. "He told me he didn't sleep with her, but he did, and now he's paying her off to keep her quiet."

She pushes me back. "Who? That reporter lady?"

I nod and put my head back on her shoulder.

"Okay," she says, rubbing my back. "Well, that sucks. He's

an asshole for lying to you, but that can't be why you're like this."

"He spent the night with me last night."

She hugs me tighter. "Oh, Soph. Did you sleep with him?"

I nod against her shoulder. "It was perfect. The entire night. He said he was falling for me and that he wanted to start a relationship. He was so sweet. And God, the sex. It was unbelievable, Mae. Everything he did and said was perfect."

"Are you sure he's lying?"

"Yeah. He told me that he'd never do anything to betray my trust, and then I get to the stadium today and find this out. He's been lying to me the whole time. I saw the bank statements. He's paying her off."

As I start bawling again, my legs give way. Maisie tries to hold me up, but I slide to the ground. She sits down and circles her arms around me.

"Breathe, Soph," she says as she starts rocking me. "You're going to be fine. You're always fine."

"Sophia." I look up to see Max walking toward us.

"Who the fuck are you?" Maisie jumps up and stands in front of me. "Back off!"

"Mae, he's security for the team. I know him."

"I don't care who he is." She pushes his chest. He doesn't budge. "Get away from her. We're handling this."

"Let me help you get her to the apartment," Max says. "That's all, then I'll leave."

"You'll leave right now," Maisie says, trying to stretch her five-foot-five frame up higher. "Come on, Sophie. Stand up. Let's get inside."

"I'm fine, Max," I say, pushing myself up.

When he tries to help me stand, Maisie punches him in the stomach. He takes a step back, smiling. "I see you're in good hands here."

Maisie puts her arm around my waist and pulls me away from him.

"Don't follow us, asshole," she yells and then lowers her voice. "You're going to be fine, Sophie. Fuck Seb. Fuck that team. Fuck everyone. I've got you, honey. You're going to be fine."

"I feel so stupid," I say as she drags me toward the door. "After Sam, I know better than to trust people. Why did I let my defenses down so quickly?"

"I don't know, Soph. Seb fooled me, too." She starts pushing me up the stairs to my apartment. "But that's done. It's time to tighten the circle. You can trust people. You trust me. And your family. And Roman—"

"Do not call Roman, Maisie," I say, turning around to look at her. "Seriously, I can't take him being involved in this right now."

"I won't call him, Soph," she whispers. "It's just me and you tonight—like it's been from the beginning. We'll get through this. Just me and you."

Chapter Thirty-Two

SEB

Manny kept his word and soared through the rest of the game. It just took two and half hours, but it felt like a lifetime. I checked my phone every time I got off the field, hoping to see a reply from Sophie. Nothing. I've sent ten texts now. Not one reply.

"After all the distraction before the game, I thought you were going to play like shit today." Bud chucks me on the shoulder. "One of your best games though. I should know better. You're always locked in."

I nod at him as I take off my equipment. I was thinking about Sophie the entire game. I barely even remember it. I was in a fog, but I guess I pulled it off.

Joe's waiting for me when I come out of the tunnel from the dugout. "She hasn't left her apartment and the friend's still there. I told Max he could leave."

"Okay, that's fine," I say. "I'll call her when I get home tonight."

Joe squints his eyes as he stares back at me. "Seems like you've calmed down a lot since the start of the game—a little too much, to be honest. What are you up to?"

"I'm not up to anything. You know playing a game always settles me down." I lean against the wall and rub my hands over my face. "Just give me some space, okay?"

Joe nods and walks about thirty feet away. That's his idea of space.

"Good game, Seb." Chick, the security guy who sits at the entrance of our clubhouse, daps me up as I walk in. "I don't know when the league's going to finally accept they can't steal second on you. Surprised you didn't break Cole's hand with that throw in the fourth. You had some extra zip tonight. Somebody must have pissed you off."

Chick's been sitting in this same chair every night for the eight years I've played here. He's well past retirement age, but the team lets him stay around. He's like a lucky charm for the players. If we don't get a fist bump from him before and after the games, I'm not sure any of us could play.

"Yeah, somebody pissed me off," I say, leaning against the wall next to him. "Hey, I need a favor from you."

He sits up straighter. "Anything, Seb."

"I need to borrow your car for the night." I lower my voice so Joe can't hear me. He's still standing well across the room from me, but he has ears like my mom.

"Naw, Seb, you don't want that," Chick laughs. "I drive a 2010 Corolla. I don't think you could fit your left thigh in there, much less your whole body."

"Actually, that sounds perfect. You want to take my Range for the night?"

"Do I want to? You know I drool over that car every time I see it." He scratches the stubble on his chin as his eyes narrow. "What are you up to, Seb? You don't let anyone get near that baby, now you want this old man to drive it."

Joe's eyeing me from across the room. I squat down next to Chick's chair. "I need to be incognito for the night."

Chick looks over my head to where Joe's standing. "Incognito from who? Joe? I noticed that he's giving you a little space tonight. You getting tired of having a shadow?"

"You have no idea."

"I know he follows you home every night. He's just doing his job, Seb. He'd get fired if anything happened to you."

"I know, Chick. I need a few hours, but I don't want you to get in trouble with him—"

"With Joe?" He throws his head back and lets out a loud laugh. "That boy ain't going to try to discipline me. I got him this damn job fifteen years ago. His daddy was my best friend all of my life."

"I didn't know that," I say, smiling. "So you're the real boss here."

"Always have been." He laughs again.

"So, do we have a deal?" I say, lowering my voice again. "Swap cars for the night?"

"How are you going to get out without Joe seeing you?"

"I'll slip out while he thinks I'm in the shower. I'm going to skip media tonight."

"You'll get fined," he says, shaking his head. "I think that's like a ten thousand dollar hit, but I guess that's chump change for you."

"It's worth it. I have to do something. I'm in a little bit of a hurry."

He crosses his arms and nods his head. "This have anything to do with that sweet, little Sophie? She came flying by me earlier. Didn't even give me a hug like she always does. She looked upset. Are you the cause of that? Don't look at me all surprised. I see everything that happens around here. I know you got it bad for her, but I have to tell you, Seb, if you upset that girl, I'm not doing anything to help you. She's a peach, that one."

"I didn't do anything to her, Chick. Believe me, I would never do that." I look up at him. His eyebrows are raised almost to his hairline. "It's a misunderstanding. I need to clear it up without a bunch of people tailing me. I need some alone time with her."

"All right, yeah, we have a deal." He reaches into his pocket and slides me his car keys. "They let me park in the stadium because I can't walk too great anymore. It's over by where the EMTs park. You know, underneath that big hotdog sign."

"Yeah, I know where it is. I'll leave my keys in my locker." I pat him on the shoulder. "I appreciate this."

"Believe me, I appreciate it way more than you do. I can't wait to drive that thing," he says, rubbing his hands together. "I promise I'll take good care of your baby."

"I know you will. I'll take care of yours, too."

"Shoot, Seb," he says, slapping my arm, "your right arm is worth a million times what my car's worth. Just make sure you stay safe. And figure out your stuff with Sophie. She's pure sunshine. I'm not sure that anyone deserves her, but you come close. I think you'd be good together."

I nod as I back away. "So do I, Chick. So do I."

As I head over to my locker, Joe walks over to Chick and starts interrogating him. I watch for a second. Chick looks over at me and winks. He's not going to give me up. I grab my clothes and Chick's keys and head toward the showers.

Our equipment guy's picking up the dirty uniforms that have been tossed on the floor. He looks up at me as I come out of the bathroom stall, fully clothed.

"You didn't see me," I say. "All right, Benji?"

He shrugs. "All right. I'm cool."

I slip around him to the back door. The security guard looks up at me and nods. "I'm going to have to tell Joe if he asks, Seb, but if he doesn't, I didn't see you either."

Chapter Thirty-Three

SOPHIE

"I'm taking your phone with me," Maisie says as she crawls out of bed. She tries to grab it, but I pull it away from her.

"I won't text him back. I promise," I say, burying the phone under the blankets. "And I need to keep it so I can text you if I change my mind about what ice cream I want."

"Sophia," she says, rolling her eyes, "when have you ever wanted any flavor other than Chunky Monkey?"

"I won't text him, Mae."

"Okay," she says as she gathers the wads of used tissues off the floor and throws them in the trash. "I'll be back in fifteen minutes and I'm checking your phone."

Seb's been texting me for hours—all during the game. Just as Maisie leaves, he tries to call me. The game must be over. He calls me a few more times. I send the calls directly to voicemail. I can't handle hearing his voice right now.

"Sophie!" His voice suddenly vibrates through my apartment. I sit straight up in bed and look around. His voice is so loud. It feels like he's right next to me.

"Sophie!" It's even louder this time and accompanied by a loud pounding noise.

It takes me a minute to realize he's at my front door. More pounding. I pull the blankets over my head.

"Sophie!" The louder he yells, the farther I burrow down into my blankets. "Sophie! Open the door. I can explain."

My phone beeps again. I peek at it. The text isn't from Seb. It's from my neighbor, Cameron. He lives across the hall.

Are you home? Some guy's trying to break down your door. I looked through my peephole, but I don't recognize him. It's not Sam. Are you ok? Do you want me to call the cops?

I throw off the blankets and jump out of bed. That's the last thing I want.

I'm good. I was sleeping. It's one of my friends. No worries. I'll let him in. Sorry to bother you, C.

I get to the door just as Seb hits it again—more softly this time.

"Soph," he says. "Please let me in. I know you're home."

"I'm not letting you in," I whisper through the door crack, "and you need to quit yelling. My neighbor wants to call the cops."

"Sophie," he says, letting out a long breath. "Thank God you're okay. Please let me in. I can explain."

I sink down the wall until I'm sitting on the floor with my

back up against the door. "You can explain with the door closed."

I hear him slide down the door. "It's not what you think."

"I think you lied to me. No, wait, I know that."

"I didn't lie to you." His voice comes in through the crack right by my face. "You know I wouldn't do that. I promised you I wouldn't and I won't. I swear."

"You slept with her and you're paying her to keep quiet." The anger's starting to rise in my voice. "I saw the bank transfers, Seb."

"Yeah." He's whispering now. I can barely hear him. "I'm paying her, but it's not for that."

"Then what's it for?"

It's quiet for about a minute before he says, "I can't tell you, Soph. I wish I could, but I can't."

I know he's lying to me. I can't believe how stupid I was to trust him. "I'm so sick of you saying that. You know trust works both ways. If you can't tell me, then you obviously don't trust me."

"I trust you so much, baby."

"Don't call me that," I say, my voice breaking.

"Soph, please let me in. I can hear you crying. It's killing me." I hear his hand running down the door. "Just please let me hold you right now, baby. That's all I want."

"I'll let you in if you tell me why you're paying her," I say, between sniffles. "If not, I want you to go away."

"She has information that could hurt me—that could hurt my family." His voice breaks a little bit. "She's blackmailing me. It makes me uncomfortable to be around her."

"What information?" I say. "Just tell me."

"Seb!" Joe's booming voice makes me jump. "What the hell?"

"Did Chick tell you where I was?" Seb sounds angry.

"That old man has never done one thing to make my job easier," Joe growls. "I saw him trying to leave in your car and stopped him. Do you have any idea where he lives? You can't have your Range Rover parked in that neighborhood. Have you lost your damn mind? Get your ass off the floor. We're leaving."

"Go away, Joe. I'm not leaving until she lets me in."

"You're leaving if I have to drag you out of here," Joe says. "Are you serious right now? We leave at seven in the morning on the last series of the season. We're a game out of first place. Get your damn head straight."

"I don't care—"

"You don't care?" I've never heard Joe sound this angry. He's usually pretty under control, but it sounds like he's about to blow. "I can give you two hundred million reasons why you should. Or are you forgetting about that contract you signed in the off-season? Get your ass off the floor. Now."

"Sophie," Seb whispers through the door crack. "I'm so sorry. It's not what you think, but I'm sorry I've caused you any pain. What can I do? I'll do anything."

"Go away, Seb. Please. That's the only thing you can do to make it better right now."

"Will you talk to me on the phone? I'll call you when I get to the car."

"No, I don't want to talk to you anymore. Just go away." I push myself off the floor. "This is making it worse, Seb. You're hurting me more. Go away. Please."

"Soph." It sounds like he's crying.

"Seb," Joe says, quieter now, "you asked me to have her back, too. We need to leave. If not for your sake, then for hers. You're hurting her. You can circle back around later but give her some space for now."

"Sophie, would it make you feel better if I left?" Seb says. He's definitely crying.

I'm so close to opening the door. I want to hold him, too. I take a quick step back.

"Yes," I say, my voice quivering. "Please go away."

"Okay, I'll give you the night, but I'm calling you tomorrow." I can tell he's still pressed up against the door. "Please pick up the phone when I call. Please."

I don't say anything, but I walk back over and lean against the door. I can almost feel his body pressed against the other side.

"Goodnight, Sophie," he whispers.

When I hear him start walking down the hall, I run back to my bedroom and dive under the blankets.

Chapter Thirty-Four

SEB

As Joe and I walk out of Sophie's apartment building, Maisie's getting out of a car. She sees me and slams the door so hard that it makes the car shake.

"What the hell are you doing here?" She runs up to me and points her finger right in my face.

"Maisie, it's not what she thinks. Please let me into her apartment so I can talk to her."

"It's not what she thinks?" She's glaring up at me. "You're paying off a woman to keep quiet about what, Seb?"

"Please let me in. I can explain," I say, grabbing her arm.

She jerks her arm away and swings her grocery bag at my chest. It lands with a hard thud.

"Jesus, Maisie. What do you have in there? Bricks?"

"Don't touch me." She swings the bag at me again but thankfully misses this time. "You're not getting anywhere near her ever again."

"Whoa, whoa, whoa." Joe steps between us, facing Maisie. "You need to settle down."

"Don't tell me what I need to do!" She's screaming. A few people are walking over—cell phones pointed at us.

Joe turns to me and nods back at the people. "We need to leave. Now."

"Maisie." She's started walking toward the apartment. "Maisie, please."

She spins around. "If you're not out of here in ten seconds, I'm calling the cops."

Joe blocks me as I try to grab her arm again.

"Right now, you're trending on Twitter for at least two days," he says. "Do you want to go for an entire week? Or maybe the lead story on the sports page? Or hell, when the cops show up, maybe you can even get some national coverage."

I watch Maisie disappear through the door.

"We have to go, Seb. You know that. Do you want to drag Sophie's name through the press? She already lost her job with the team, but if you make this a story, she's going to lose her whole goddamn business. Walk away—for her."

I take a deep breath and nod as I start toward Chick's car.

"No." Joe grabs my shoulder. "You're riding with me. Max and Henry took the Range Rover to your house. They're headed over here to get Chick's car."

He clicks his locks and opens the door for me. I think I see him shove a few people back away from me. I'm not sure. My mind's not working right now.

I'm staring at my phone when he gets in the car. He takes it from me and puts it on the dashboard.

"Give it a rest, Seb," he says, starting the car. "Leave her alone."

"Did you say she lost her job with the team?"

"Yeah," he says. "Gary fired her. Well, I think she quit first, but she's gone either way."

"Because of me?"

"Gary said he fired her because she was sleeping with you, but I think it was really because she beat up Gentry." He shakes his head and laughs. "Apparently before we got there, she gave him an elbow to the eye and a crushing blow to the balls."

"That's not funny, Joe. I should have been there to protect her."

"From Gentry?" He laughs again. "She doesn't need any help against that weak, little bitch. My five-year-old could kick his ass."

I'm still not finding any of this funny. "Did Gentry touch her?"

"Gary says the attack was unprovoked, so yeah, I'm guessing he touched her. Gary isn't big on the truth where his family's concerned."

"I'm going to fucking kill him."

He turns to look at me when we pull up at a stoplight. "You're going to do what you need to do, but there are better ways to take Gentry down."

"Meaning?"

"Gentry has a pattern of this behavior. The team's been hiding it for years." He's staring at me. His eyes aren't blinking. "Maybe it's time for the world to know."

"And how does the world find out about it? Sophie mentioned it to me, but she said no one had proof."

"There's proof." He looks away. "We just need to find someone with the balls to take Gary on. He ruins careers."

"If he comes after Sophie, I'm going to take him down. I don't care what I have to do. I'll lose my entire career to protect her. I know you don't understand that, but it's just the way I feel."

He doesn't say anything. We drive in silence for about fifteen minutes before he finally says, "When I met Darcy, I knew. I mean the second I met her. She started talking and a little voice inside me told me I was going to marry her. It never happened with another woman. I dated some great women before her, but I never heard that voice. Are you hearing that voice now?"

"From the second I saw her." I turn to look at him. "God, I think I'm in love with her. How's that even possible? I just met her."

"It's possible," he says, sighing. "It happened to me. It happens all of the time."

"Did it happen for Darcy that fast?"

He smiles. "We disagree about that. She says no, but I know she was at least really into me at first sight. It might not have been love for her right away, but it didn't take very long. We were engaged after only five months. Have I ever told you that?"

"No." I smile for the first time tonight. "That's cool. And you've been married ten years?"

"Yeah, eleven in December. I'd be an entirely different person if I hadn't met her. It happens like that sometimes."

"Sophie doesn't feel the same way I do. She didn't before today and now she definitely doesn't. She hates me."

"She doesn't hate you," he says. "She's confused. She knows you're hiding something from her. She doesn't know what it is and it's hurting her."

"I want to tell her," I say, looking out the window again, "but it's not mine to tell. You know?"

"Yeah, I know. You can't tell her."

After Joe drops me off at the house, I pace around the kitchen for about an hour before I finally text her again.

Sophie, please talk to me. You're all I care about right now. Nothing else matters. Just you.

I throw my phone back on the counter and grab another beer out of the refrigerator. My heart stops when I hear my phone ping. I run over and grab it.

I know you care about me and I know you don't want to hurt me. But that's what you're doing. If you want to stop hurting me, please leave me alone.

An intense pain shoots through my body. I stare at her text for a few minutes before I reply.

Ok. I'll leave you alone. I promise. I'm so sorry for hurting you.

I toss and turn all night—checking my phone every ten minutes. There's no reply. Finally, I hear a ping about five in the morning. I almost dive off the bed to grab it. It's a text from Joe.

Hey. I have some family stuff to take care of this morning. Max is going to pick you up. I'll fly down to meet the team later today.

Chapter Thirty-Five

SOPHIE

Maisie forced me to leave my bed this morning to get coffee. I only agreed because I knew Seb wouldn't be waiting outside my apartment. The team left this morning for their last road trip of the season.

I'm sitting at a table outside while she gets our lattes. The sun feels so good on my face. I'm starting to relax a little bit when I see Joe walking toward my table.

"Shouldn't you be with the team?" I say, glaring at him.

"I'm headed that way in about an hour. I had something to do first."

"He shouldn't have sent you here." My voice breaks as I feel the tears start to well up in my eyes again.

"He didn't send me. He doesn't know I'm here." Joe sits down in the chair opposite of me as I stand up. "Sophie, sit your ass down in that chair right now or I will help you. I'm well beyond tired of all of this."

I sit down slowly as he peers over the top of his sunglasses at me with the look he usually reserves for overly aggressive fans.

"No!" Maisie comes out of the coffee shop, carrying the lattes. She stops inches from Joe. I'm more than a little worried that she's about to pour coffee on his head. "If you don't get the hell out of here, we're leaving."

Joe looks from her to me. "Sophie, I have information that I think you want."

"I don't want to talk about it, Joe." I cross my arms and scoot my chair back from the table. Maisie's still standing over him.

"Good, then you can just listen." He takes off his sunglasses and rubs his eyes. "But I need you alone. She can sit across the patio and watch my every move."

"No!" Maisie puts my coffee on the table and shoves him on the shoulder. He looks up at her and shakes his head.

"You're a feisty little thing for your size. Let me know if you ever want a job in security."

Maisie starts taking the top off of her coffee.

"Mae!" I say, jumping in front of her. "Do not throw that coffee on him. Give us five minutes."

"Five minutes." She puts her hand in his face. "The clock just started."

He watches her walk to the other side of the patio before he starts. "He'll kill me for telling you this—"

"Then don't tell me."

"I thought you weren't going to talk."

I roll my eyes and look away from him.

"Seb's mom spent some time in jail in her early twenties."

"What?" I say, looking back at him. He's looking down.

219

"Yeah, nothing violent or anything. White-collar stuff," he sighs. "She did some stupid things—insider trading. She broke the law and spent almost two years in jail. Apparently, her time in jail was pretty traumatic for her. She still suffers from a little PTSD."

I take a deep breath. "I had no idea. Seb never said anything."

"He didn't know about it until a few months ago. It's still new to him." He starts rubbing his temples. "Liza Murray found out. She wanted to write a story on it. Seb's been paying her off to keep it quiet, so his mom doesn't have to relive it publicly."

"What? That's blackmail." My heart's sinking in my chest. "Oh my God. Why hasn't he told anyone?"

"He did. He told me. I told Ken. We asked that Liza have her media credential taken away—for obvious reasons. Ken said he'd take care of her. She was banned for about a week. That's when she threatened to sue the team, then all of a sudden, she got her credential back like nothing happened. I think she has something on the Randalls, too."

"Liza told me Seb slept with her and was paying her off to keep quiet."

He shakes his head. "Sophie, Seb did not sleep with her. Not his type at all. I've been around him for years. He's only dated a few women in that time, and he was insanely private about those relationships. He would never date someone he works with because it would be too public."

He holds up his hand to stop my protest.

"Except you, but that's only because he's crazy about you.

I mean, absolutely insane. I've never seen him lose it over someone like this."

I take a long drink of my latte as I try to piece it all together. "Why do you think Liza told me all of that? It doesn't make sense."

"Yeah, it does, and that's part two of our conversation." He slides the folder that he's been holding across the table.

I don't touch it. "What is it?"

"Harassment complaints about Gentry including one from Liza."

He sees my confused face.

"Yeah," he says. "Gentry harassed her, too."

"What? They're so close. Why does she hang out with him if he did that?"

"She's getting money from Gary, too, to keep quiet about Gentry." He looks up at me again. "She lets Gentry think that she's cool with him, so she can pump him for information about the team. Bottom line, I think she's going to write about all of this at some point."

"How did she find out about Seb's mom?"

"Seb's uncle sold the information to Liza. Crazy, right? Everybody tries to cash in on fame. Seb didn't even know about it until Liza approached him. His little sister still doesn't know about it."

I take a deep breath. "That's why he doesn't want to talk about it? Because of his sister?"

"Yeah, his mom made him swear he wouldn't tell anyone. She doesn't want her daughter to know. She didn't want Seb to know either. It crushed her when he found out. Frankly, I think she should tell the sister. It's probably going to come out at some point. It seems like it would be better if she heard it from her mom, but that's not my business."

I open the file and start leafing through it. "It looks like all the complaints are about something Gentry said—verbal harassment. Has it gone beyond that?"

"You tell me. Did it go beyond that last night?"

"He put his hand on my butt, but I took care of him."

"That's what I understand. Gentry was on the floor when we came in. Did you do that?"

I nod.

"I might have a job for you on my security team, too." He smiles. "I have to go or I'll be late for my flight. I wanted you to know this before I left. Seb's a good guy and he's crazy about you. He's just trying to protect his mom from all of this blowing up. He doesn't want her to have to deal with everything again."

He starts to walk away, leaving the folder on the table.

"You forgot something," I say, holding it up.

"No, I didn't. That's yours now." He turns back to me. "I know I should have come forward with all of this a long time ago, but I don't have the balls. I need my job. I hope you have more courage than I do."

"If I do something with this, they're going to know I got it from you. Who else would have access to it?"

He shrugs. "Yeah, probably. I'm not sure what to do anymore. Maybe it would be better if I got fired. I don't know. The folder's yours. Do what you want with it."

"Joe, I think I misjudged you. I thought you were a part of this—"

"You didn't misjudge me," he says, taking a deep breath.

"I wasn't an active part of it, but I didn't do anything to stop it either. Look, bottom line—Seb's a good guy. Give him a chance. I think you'd be good together."

Ray's editor told me that I'd find him across the street from the newspaper's offices, sitting on a park bench. Apparently, that's where he eats his lunch. It's been three days since Joe gave me the information. It's taken me that long to decide what to do with it.

"Well, Sophia Banks," Ray says as I slide onto the park bench beside him, "I thought I might see you again. You didn't make it on the last road trip. Rumor is that you were canned."

"Yeah, I quit or I was fired. I'm not sure, but I don't work with the team anymore."

"Do you want to explain to me—on the record—why that is? And why Gentry has a black eye? Someone told me you gave it to him."

"Sure," I say, laughing. "I'll go on the record. Are you ready?"

He pops out his phone and turns on the recorder. "I'm always ready."

"Gentry found out that I had a personal relationship with a player. He threatened to tell his dad and get me fired. He said he wouldn't tell if he and I made an arrangement. He put his hand on my butt. I elbowed him hard in the eye and kicked him even harder in the crotch. I told him if he ever touched me again, he was going to lose an arm. I left. I resigned the account. End of story."

Ray clicks off the recorder. "You know if I print that, you're going to lose a lot of clients."

"Maybe, but I think I'll pick up some new clients—the right kind." I shrug. "And if I don't, then it might be time to find another career. I handled the situation the right way. He was way over the line. I don't have time for bullshit like that. No one should. He needs to be publicly shamed."

"Unfortunately, I don't think that one incident is enough of a story. Do you know of anyone else who would go on the record?"

I pull the folder out of my bag and place it between us on the bench.

"And what is that?" he asks, eyeing it.

"It's five other women who Gentry harassed. They filed official complaints with the team, but Gary buried them. No one who works for the team will cross him. They're scared of losing their jobs. I've only talked to one of them. She's willing to go on the record. You'll have to ask the others yourself."

"Who's willing to go on the record?" He picks up the folder.

"The first one." As he flips the folder open, I point to the first name.

"Liza Murray?" He glances over at me, a confused look on his face.

"Yep. Long story, short, she knows something potentially damaging about a player's family member—"

"What? The story about Seb's mom? That she did time?"

I try to hide my surprise. "You know about that?"

"I've known about it since Liza found out. We shared the same editor at the paper. Liza pitched the story to her. Our editor turned it down because she didn't think it was newsworthy. I mean, it happened decades ago. It was an insider trading thing—illegal, but not really all that interesting. Liza wanted to report it from an angle of Seb growing up with a hardened criminal. It wasn't a story. Our editor told Liza to not pursue it. She did anyway. She approached Seb. I don't think Seb even knew about it until then."

"He didn't."

"Yeah, I figured. The PR staff lost their minds—came down hard on our editor. She fired Liza. I didn't ask why, but I knew that was the reason. I always figured there was more to the story. What is it?"

"You'll have to talk to her further, but basically, she told me when she was kicked out of the clubhouse, Gentry offered to get her back in if she slept with him. She went right to Gary and threatened to sue. Gary reinstated her credentials and has been paying her to keep quiet."

"She's willing to go on the record about the payoff?"

"She said she was," I say, leaning back on the bench and closing my eyes. "I think she feels bad about it—wants to come clean."

"Is Seb paying her, too, so she'll keep quiet about his mom?" He pauses for a second. "His mom doing time is not a story, but him paying off Liza s, especially as it relates to the bigger picture of Gentry. I'd have to include it in the story."

When I open my eyes, he's staring down at me. I shrug. "Seb didn't tell me that."

"That's a good non-answer, Sophia. Who did tell you that?"

"I've told you what I'm going to tell you. Anything else is

between you and Seb. What Gentry and Gary are doing is wrong. I hope you report on the story because the harassment needs to end."

"Have you talked to Seb about this?"

"I haven't talked to him since the night I left the team."

"I'm guessing he's the one you have the personal relationship with—"

"Had."

"Why had?" He looks at me with concern in his eyes. "Did he do something to you?"

"No. I did something to him. I didn't trust him to be the person he showed me he was. I'm guessing he doesn't want much to do with me anymore."

"And I'm guessing you're completely wrong about that."

"Maybe," I say, standing up. "I have to leave. My best friend's getting married in Chicago this weekend. We're flying out there today. She'll kill me if I miss the plane."

"Okay, Sophia," he says, smiling. "I'm going to miss you."

"What? We're apart for a couple of days and you're already forgetting about me," I say, laughing.

"Oh I'm guessing once someone meets Sophia Banks, they don't forget about her too soon." He reaches for my hand and squeezes it. "And that includes Seb. Call him. I've known him a long time. I've never seen him as happy as when you're around."

I lean over and hug him. "Bye, Ray. On the record, I think you're the sweetest reporter I've ever met."

"Definitely don't tell anyone else that," he chuckles as I walk away. "Really bad for my reputation."

Chapter Thirty-Six

SEB

We missed the playoffs by one game. Usually, that would gnaw at me for months after the season, but I pretty much stopped thinking about it a minute after the final pitch.

The only thing on my mind is Sophie. I promised I would leave her alone, and I have. It's been agony. Every time my phone rings, my heart skips a beat, hoping it's her, and then sinks to my toes when it's not. Right now is no different. I lunge for my phone as it goes off. It's Ray Franklin.

"What?" I growl into the phone. "I gave you my post-season interview. I don't want to talk about it anymore."

"This isn't about the season, Seb. I'm publishing a story on Saturday about Gentry Randall. Specifically about his inappropriate behavior toward female team employees. I have five women going on the record for the story. One of them is Liza Murray."

"Liza? Going on the record about Gentry?"

"Yeah. After the team pulled her credentials, Gentry

offered to get them back if she'd sleep with him. She has a recording. It's going to be damning for him."

"Wow," I say, shaking my head. "I had no idea. I'm sorry that happened to her. I'm not sure what it has to do with me, though."

"Part of the story is why she got her credentials pulled in the first place." He pauses, but I know what's coming next. I close my eyes. "I know about your mom. I have for a long time. That alone isn't a story, but the fact that you're paying Liza not to write about it—that's part of the story. Liza confirmed that you were. I'm sorry, Seb. I wanted to give you a heads up."

I take a deep breath. "Okay. I'll let my family know."

"Do you want to be quoted in the story?"

I take a few more deep breaths as I think about it. He waits.

"Yeah, here's your quote. My mom is one of the best people in the world. She's had my back since the day I was born. I hate that my job is making her relive a painful part of her life, but she's the strongest person I know. She'll get through it. And I'm going to make sure of it because I will always have her back, too."

I hang up without waiting for his reply. I like Ray. I know he's just doing his job, but that's the first and only thing I'm ever going to say publicly about this. I try to clear my thoughts before I call Mom.

"Hey, honey!" The sound of her voice always cheers me up, but not today. I feel awful about what I have to tell her.

"Hey, Mom."

"We have the lake house all ready for you. Are you still coming up tomorrow?"

"Yeah," I say. "I was planning on it."

"What do you mean 'planning on it'? Oh honey, are you still sad about the way the season ended? Seb, you had one of your best seasons. You did everything you could."

"Mom, I have to tell you something."

"You can tell me anything." Her voice gets quieter. "You know that. What's wrong, Seb?"

I close my eyes. "The Miami newspaper's going to print a story about your time in jail."

She exhales loudly. "Seb, we were going to wait until you were back here to tell you, but your dad and I told your sister about my jail time the other night. We guessed it was going to come out at some point. We wanted her to hear it from us."

"I'm so sorry, Mom."

"About what?" Her voice gets indignant when someone's trying to challenge one of her kids. "This is not your fault, Sebastian. I should have been open with you about this from the beginning. I made a mistake. I paid for it. I don't want to relive that horrible time, but it is what it is. None of this is your fault. I feel awful that you're ashamed."

"Mom," I say. "God, I'm not ashamed of you. You're the best mom in the world. I don't want you to be hurt by this. Your friends are going to find out and it's going to bring all the trauma back."

"Seb, I'm fine. I have the best support system in the world. Some people are going to talk. They always do, but as long as you and Mady are okay with it, it doesn't matter what other people think."

"Mady's okay with it?"

"You know how your sister is—the champion of the oppressed and the downtrodden. I think it's made her like me more."

"Yeah, probably," I say, laughing. "I love you, Mom."

"I love you, too, honey—more than anything in the world. You could never do anything to disappoint me. Get yourself to Michigan. We'll hunker down for a while until it blows over. It always does."

"Okay. Is the house key in the same place?"

"Still under the ceramic frog by the hydrangeas," she says, laughing. "We'll be down next week—probably Tuesday. Are you bringing that woman you like? What's her name? Sophie?"

My heart skips a beat again. "Uh, no, I think that's probably done."

"What? You told me you really liked her."

"I do, but I kind of messed it up."

"I doubt that." She's indignant again. It makes me smile. I definitely got my fierce protective nature from her.

"Mom, I do make mistakes sometimes."

"I'm not sure how that can be when you're perfect. And if this Sophie can't see that, that's her problem."

I laugh. "We can talk about it next week. Okay? I need to pack and take care of some stuff here before I leave. I love you, Mom."

"I love you, too, honey. We can't wait to see you."

When I hang up, I call Joe.

"Hey. Are you still going to Michigan tomorrow?"

"Yeah. Ray Franklin called me. He's printing a story about

Gentry on Saturday. It's going to include Mom's jail time. Did you have anything to do with that story getting out? I'm not mad if you did. It was going to come out at some point."

"I didn't talk to Ray directly about it, but I provided the information to someone else—"

"Sophie?"

"Yeah."

"Okay, will you keep an eye on her while I'm gone? I promised I wouldn't contact her. I'm not going to break that promise. I'm worried that Gary's going to come after her, though. I'll call her friend Roman, too. He'll protect her, but check on her to make sure she's okay."

"I've got you." He pauses for a second. "If you don't want me to head your detail anymore, I'll understand."

"There are only so many people who can put up with me, Joe, and you're one of them. Don't think you're getting off the hook that easily. You're stuck with me."

Chapter Thirty-Seven

SOPHIE

When I peek into Maisie's room, all I see are mounds of blankets and pillows on the bed. It's her wedding day. We shared a suite at the hotel last night. I check the bathroom to see if she's in there. Nothing. For a second, I think we might have a runaway bride situation.

"I'm hiding." I hear her whisper. I see the blankets move a little bit.

I lift them to see her curled in a fetal position in the center of the bed.

"Hiding from whom?" I say, laughing.

"Not who, what."

I crawl under with her. "What? Are you having second thoughts?"

"About Ryan, definitely not. About this entire day, yes."

"Yeah, I get that," I say, pulling her into a snuggle. "It's a lot."

"I can't wait to get this day over with and be in Hawaii already," she whispers. "Does that sound horrible?"

"No," I say, laying my head on her shoulder. "It's the way I would feel. You know I'm horrified by big weddings."

"Yeah, but only because you don't want all of the attention on you. I love attention. I'm just worried that something's not going to go right and Mom's going to lose her mind. She's been texting me since five."

"What?" I crawl out from under the blankets and grab her phone off the nightstand. "This phone's mine for the rest of the day. Melinda has to deal with me from now on."

"She's going to drive you crazy. You know what a perfectionist she is."

"Something will go wrong. It always does." I squeeze her hand. "But that's why you have me here. Any problems are the responsibility of the Maid of Honor. Your only responsibility is to have fun."

She finally surfaces out of the blankets and lays her head on the pillows. "God, I can't wait to do this for you when you get married. I'm going to spoil you so badly."

"Don't hold your breath. I think Savannah was probably right. It's not going to happen for me until I'm at least fifty."

"Savannah is never right about anything." She shoves my shoulder. "Don't let me hear you say something so ridiculous again."

"You're right, but enough talk about me. It's your day, princess. What can I do for you this morning?"

"Call Seb."

"Mae, what did I just say?" I look up at her, shaking my head. "No more talk about me."

"Excuse me," she says, smiling. "It's my day. I can talk about whatever I want. Call him."

"He doesn't want to hear from me."

"You don't know that."

"Mae," I say, closing my eyes. "I believed the worst about him when he gave me no reason to do so. He was perfect from the first second I met him and I couldn't trust him."

"Sweetie, you had every reason not to trust him. I mean, I understand why he couldn't tell you about his mom, but he knew you had trust issues. He had to know that hiding anything from you wasn't going to work."

"Yeah, I guess. But I should have understood. I hide secrets all the time for my clients."

Her phone beeps. I pull it away from her.

"Melinda wants to know if you confirmed the gluten-free meals."

"Seriously? I swear she asked me that yesterday. Give me the phone."

"No." I pull it farther away from her. "I'll text her back."

I jump out of bed, so she can't stop me and send a quick text.

Hey Mel. It's Sophie. I've taken over Mae's phone for the rest of the day. She's confirmed everything. Time for you to relax and have fun.

I show the text to Maisie. She throws her hands over her eyes.

"Eek! You're in trouble now, Sophia," she says as she burrows back under the blankets.

The phone beeps.

Sophie, you're like a daughter to me, but don't think I won't come up there right now and slap you. It is a mother's job to worry and I excel at it.

I read the text to Maisie.

"Well, you can't say Mom doesn't have great self-aware-ness. Don't text her back. Maybe if we ignore her, she'll stop."

"Melinda never stops. If we don't text back, she'll be up here in a few minutes."

"Let her try to get in. She doesn't have a key." She pulls me back into the bed. "I read the story on the Randalls this morning. It sounds devastating for them. There's even talk of prosecution."

"Why are you reading that crap on your wedding day?"

"Because I'm worried about you." She hugs me tighter. "They have to know you were the source. Have they tried to contact you?"

I shake my head against her shoulder. "I blocked their numbers. And Roman's chomping at the bit to get involved. I'm not sure how he even found out that I was the leak. Did you tell him?"

"Absolutely not. I promised you I wouldn't talk to him anymore about BFF secrets."

"Well, I told him I'd call him if the Randalls tried to contact me."

"I'm guessing that Roman—and his brothers—have already told them not to contact you."

I sigh. "I asked him not to approach them, but you know how he gets."

"So you think it's going to affect your business?"

"It's going to kill my business. Even if the Randalls don't tell people I was the leak, everyone will know. No company's going to hire me after I've broken a non-disclosure."

"Maybe—"

"No, Mae," I say, "I'm okay with it. Like really okay. I'm tired of teaching grown men how to behave properly. You know? I think it's time for them to go down with their ships."

"What are you going to do now?" she says, stroking my hair.

"I don't know. I'll think of something. You know I always land on my feet." I reluctantly crawl out of bed. "Do you want a Starbucks? I'll do a run as one of my last official duties as Maid of Honor."

"Yes, but first you have to promise me something." She peers at me over the top of the blankets. Her eyes are getting mischievous. "After my wedding's over, you have to call Seb —if only to apologize."

"Maisie—"

"Stop!" She points her finger at me. "I'm playing my bride card."

"Oh my God," I say, rolling my eyes. "You've been playing that card for about eighteen months now. Your reign is over, Bridezilla."

"It's over when I say 'I do,' but I can still use it this morning. Promise me you'll call him after the wedding."

"Fine," I say, throwing a pillow at her. "I'll be back with your latte in a few minutes, Your Highness."

"If you're not, I'm sending out a search party. And I'm not letting you out of my sight for the rest of the day."

"You don't trust me to make it to the ceremony on time, do you?"

"Not even a little bit, honey," she says, smiling. "You know I've always had to push you. If it wasn't for me, I don't know that you'd ever get to where you're meant to be. Now give me my phone back. I have to take care of a few things before I can have fun."

Chapter Thirty-Eight

SEB

I made it to Michigan yesterday. Usually, by this time, I'm out on the water, fishing, but I can't find enough energy to even do that. All I've been able to do is sit on the back porch and stare out at the lake.

Sophie's still the only thing on my mind. I've been looking at my phone for days, trying to get the nerve up to text her. That's pretty much all I've been doing since I walked away from her apartment about a week ago.

She made it clear that she didn't want to talk to me, but I want to talk to her. I want to tell her about my mom. Tell her about everything—forever. I want to start talking and not stop until I've told her every single little thing that's ever happened to me in my life. And then I want her to start talking and never stop.

Joe texted me a link this morning to a story about the Randalls. It reveals all their unsavory business dealings—

focusing on a long string of payouts to women Gentry has harassed. Sophie was the source of that story and I'm worried about her. I want to protect her from them and from any person who tries to hurt her. I asked Joe to check on her. He said she's out of town. He doesn't know where.

I type "Can we talk?" into my phone for about the hundredth time. It's the best I've been able to come up with. I'm trying to convince myself to push send when a text pops up from a strange number.

It's Maisie. Just FYI, Joe told Sophie about your mom. I'm sorry you had to go through that. Sophie feels awful about not trusting you. I told her to call you, but she doesn't think you'll want to talk to her. I'm guessing that's not the case…

Also, sorry about hitting you in the chest with my grocery bag. It was ice cream, by the way, not bricks. Chunky Monkey. It's Sophie's favorite flavor if you want to tuck that away for the future.

I'm getting married tonight in Chicago. Reception starts around 7pm at The Peninsula. Sophie doesn't have a date. I know it's late notice, but I'm wondering if there's something you can do about that, Sep!!??!

I jump out of my chair so quickly that I knock my coffee onto the deck. I text her back immediately.

All I want to do is talk to her. That's all I can think about. Headed your way. I might be late, but I'll be there.

And, no worries about the ice cream, but maybe go with soft serve next time. I still have a bruise on my chest.

As I run to the bedroom to grab my suitcase, I call Mom.

"Hey, honey!" She sounds cheerful. I'm guessing she hasn't read the story yet.

"Hey, Mom." I take a deep breath and exhale slowly. "The story ran today."

"I know. We've already read it." She sighs. "At least it's fair. It doesn't make me out to be any worse—or better—than I am."

"Has anyone called you yet?"

"Not yet, but I'm guessing the sharks are going to start circling at some point. Everyone likes a scandal. We're thinking about heading to the lake today. Is that okay with you? Or do you need some alone time?"

"That's part of why I'm calling you," I say. "Sophie's best friend just texted me. She's getting married in Chicago today and invited me to her wedding."

"The friend invited you?" She pauses for a second. "Does Sophie know you're coming?"

"I'm not sure," I say, shoving my clothes into the suitcase. "I haven't texted her because I don't want her to tell me not to come."

"Do you think that's the best approach?"

"I've got to talk to her, Mom. I think I might be in love with her. I've never felt this way." I sit on the bed and take a few deep breaths. "Am I doing the right thing?"

"Honey, I've never heard you this stressed out. You're usually so calm about everything. You need to talk to her. Just go and worry about the rest later."

"Okay, I'm not sure when I'll be back. I'm sorry I'm leaving you right when everything's blowing up."

"Seb, I'll be fine. Your dad and I will take care of each other like we always do. We'll hang out when you get back. Leave the key under the frog. And if you work things out with Sophie, bring her back to Michigan. We'd love to meet her."

"Okay. I will. I love you, Mom."

The four-hour drive to Chicago felt like it took four days, but now that I'm pulling up to the hotel, I wish that it had taken a little longer. I've been trying to figure out what to say to Sophie, but I haven't come up with anything great yet.

"Hey," the valet says, squinting his eyes, "you look just like Seb Miller."

"Yeah, I get that a lot." I crawl out of the car and hand him the keys. "I'm not a big sports fan. He plays football, right?"

"Baseball," he laughs. "He's the catcher in Miami."

"Cool. Well, at least he has a nice place to play."

He hands me the valet stub. "Are you sure you're not him?"

I grab the pen out of his shirt pocket and autograph the stub.

"Keep the car close, okay?" I say, handing him a hundred.

"Nice." He nods his head and smiles. "I'm a Cubs' fan. Why do you always have to beat up on us so much?"

"There's something about Wrigley, brother." I chuck him on the shoulder. "Keep it close. I might be out of here in a few minutes."

"You got it, Seb."

I try to keep my head low as I walk through the lobby to the concierge.

"Hey. I'm looking for a wedding. First name of the bride is Maisie."

He looks up and smiles. "Yes, the Clarkson/Monroe wedding. Grand Ballroom. It's marked on the elevator."

As I get off the elevator, I walk into the ballroom just in time to see Maisie—in the fluffiest wedding dress I've ever seen—yelling at a group of people. She's pointing a bunch of flowers at them. I walk a little bit farther into the room and see Sophie in the group. She's wearing a pink, silky long dress that's clinging to every stunning curve of her body. Her hair's flowing down her back in a mass of curls. She looks so beautiful that I almost can't breathe.

"Sophie!" Maisie yells, pointing the flowers at her. "Quit being a coward! This is meant for you and only you."

Sophie grabs some young girls and pulls them in front of her. It looks like she's using them as human shields.

"You can't make me do anything! Your bridal card expired the minute you said, 'I do.' Remember?" Sophie says, ducking down behind the kids.

Maisie turns around briefly—her back to the group—but then whips around and throws the flowers right at Sophie. Sophie puts her hands over her head. I jump forward and catch the flowers just before they hit her.

Chapter Thirty-Nine

SOPHIE

"Sophie!" Maisie points at me with her bouquet. "Quit being a coward! This is meant for you, and only you."

It's time for the most-dreaded wedding tradition—the bridal bouquet toss. I'm the last of our close group of girlfriends to get married, so all of the attention is on me. I hate it. I tried to hide, but Taylor and Savannah pulled me onto the floor. It's me, a few women I've never seen, and a collection of little girls. Maisie points at me again—her eyebrows raised.

"You can't make me do anything!" I say as I grab Maisie's eight-year-old niece and try to hide behind her. "Your bridal card expired the minute you said, 'I do.' Remember?"

Maisie scowls at me and turns around, so her back's facing us. She acts like she's going to toss the bouquet over her shoulder, then she whips back around, takes a few quick steps toward me, and throws it right at my face. I cover my head with my hands, but just before it hits me, someone grabs it. I look up to see Seb standing in front of me, holding the bouquet.

I look quickly from the flowers to his eyes. "What are you doing here?"

"Well apparently, I have to follow you around the country to keep you from getting hit in the head with flying objects." He lifts the bouquet up to emphasize his point. "I taught you how to catch, Sophie."

"I didn't want to catch that," I say, backing up a few steps.

"I could tell," he says, shaking his head. "Are you scared of flowers, too?"

"Just those flowers. The person who catches the bridal bouquet is supposed to be the one who gets married next."

He smiles. "So I'm getting married next?"

"I think it might only apply to single females."

He nods and looks down at my fellow competitors. He sees the three-year-old flower girl looking longingly at the bouquet.

"Hey," he says, squatting down and smiling at her. "Do want to catch these flowers?"

She nods, looking from him to the flowers, her eyes getting wider.

"Okay, do you know how to catch? When I throw them, trap them against your chest like this." He tosses them in the air and traps them against his chest to show her. "Are you ready?"

He leans closer to her and gently tosses them. She closes her eyes as she throws her arms around them.

Seb looks up at me and laughs. "She catches just like you."

"Good job!" he says as she opens her eyes. After he pats

her on the head, he stands back up and looks at me. "She's, what, about three? So if she's the next one married, you have at least twenty years before you have to worry about it."

He looks around the room. Everyone's staring at him, as usual. He grabs my hand.

"Come here," he says, pulling me toward the ballroom door.

I look over my shoulder. Maisie's grinning at me.

"Was this you?" I mouth to her.

She shrugs and smiles. I shake my head and smile back at her. My best friend is perfect.

When Seb gets me out in the hallway, he pulls me behind a row of planters. "Maisie said you didn't have a date to the wedding. Is that true?"

"Yeah," I say, nodding.

"Do you want one?" He points down to his jeans. "I drove over here from the lake house, so I don't have wedding clothes—"

I throw myself into his chest and wrap my arms around his waist. "I missed you so much."

"God, I missed you, too," he whispers as he wraps his arms around me. He rests his chin on top of my head. "Every second. It was agony."

He pushes me against the wall and leans into me as he takes a hungry kiss.

He pulls his lips back a couple of inches. "I promised my mom I wouldn't tell anyone, but I should have told you."

"No, you shouldn't have. I should have trusted you," I whisper. "I'm so sorry, Seb."

He kisses me again—more gently this time—and then

pulls me back into a hug. "You never have to apologize to me for anything. Never."

I nod against his chest.

"Were you Ray Franklin's source for that story?" he asks.

I nod again. "I'm sorry, Seb. I didn't want your mom to be part of it, but the stuff about Gentry needed to get out."

"What did I just say? You didn't do anything wrong. No apologies."

I rest my head on his chest. "Is your mom okay?"

"My mom's tough. She'll be fine. The main thing that's on her mind right now is meeting this Sophie woman I've been telling her so much about."

"You told your mom about me?" I finally smile. His eyes are starting to light up.

"All about you, including how strong you are." He lets his hands slide down my arms until he's holding my hands. "The Randalls are threatening Joe. They suspect he's the source of the story."

"I'll tell them I was the one who gave it to Ray. I don't want Joe to lose his job."

"Absolutely not. Joe will be fine. I'll make sure of that." He squeezes my hands. "Promise me you won't talk to them."

"I promise." I laugh as he raises his eyebrows. "Really, I promise. I won't. I've already blocked their numbers."

"Okay." He puts his arms around me and pulls me tightly to him again. "Tell me if they try to contact you. I'm not going to let anyone hurt you. I told you that before. And if they try to ruin your reputation, I'll kill them."

"I'm not even worried about it," I say, rubbing my cheek

against his chest. I've missed it so much. "All I've been worried about is you and your family."

"My family is fine."

"Oh no, speaking of family . . ." I push him back and point to my brothers who are closing in on us like vultures.

"Uh, Soph," my brother, Luke, yells as he runs up to us with our other brother, Jake, right on his heels, as usual. "Why didn't you tell us you were friends with Seb Miller?"

They're both looking up at Seb like they're seeing the face of God. I push them both in their chests. "Why were you whispering my name during the wedding ceremony like complete lunatics? How old are you?"

They ignore me. Jake taps Luke and points toward Seb's arms around my waist. "It looks like they're a little more than friends."

They both laugh like twelve-year-olds and pulse their eyebrows up and down. I try to hit them again, but Seb pulls me back.

"Seb, these are my idiot big brothers—Dumber and Dumbest."

"Oh," Seb says. "So these are the two whose asses I get to kick."

"Wait, what?" Luke takes a quick step back, almost knocking Jake over.

"Yeah," Seb says, tightening his arms around me. "I understand that you threw a football at her head when she was five."

"That has never been proven!" Jake points at me from behind Luke.

"And then you kept throwing stuff at her while you were growing up?"

"Sophie! Why are you telling my idol lies about me?" Luke grabs his chest and tries to act shocked. "You're just mad because you weren't born with any athletic talent."

"I wouldn't be so sure about that," Seb says, kissing the top of my head. "I taught her how to catch, and she already has a mean, little fastball. You might be surprised the next time you throw something at her. Of course, if I'm around, I'm going to be the one to throw the ball back to you. And it's going right at your head. I'm pretty accurate from at least a couple hundred feet."

Jake looks up at him, eyes wide. "You're the most accurate catcher ever. Your throw to second is perfect every time. You're perfect. You rarely make an error, and you never have a passed ball. Please be my best friend, Seb Miller. Please. I swear Luke made me throw the ball at her."

Luke backhands him across the chest. "It was all Jake's idea," he says, looking up at Seb with the same wide eyes. "You really taught her how to catch?"

"I really did." Seb squeezes me tighter.

Luke looks at me, shaking his head. "I've never been more jealous of you in my life, and that includes the time Mom and Dad took you to Great America and left us at home because we buried Mr. BunBun in the backyard."

Seb laughs and tilts my head up to look at him. "Do I want to know who Mr. BunBun is?"

"My stuffed rabbit. Sadly, he never recovered from the trauma of that day."

"Well it looks like you two have ganged up on Sophie her entire life," Seb says. "Just know that I'm on her team now, and I take winning very seriously. I don't take prisoners."

"I would be happy to be your prisoner—"

"Shut up, you weirdo." I push Jake into Luke. "You're both out of control. Stop fanboying all over him. He's just a guy."

"The best guy ever created." Jake reaches over to touch Seb's arm. "I just touched Seb Miller's throwing arm."

"What is wrong with you?" I swat Jake's arm away and look up at Seb. "I'm so sorry. I'd like to tell you they get more tolerable, but they don't. And my dad's going to be even worse."

"I'll live," Seb says, putting his hand under my chin. "If they're the price I have to pay to be with you, I'll gladly pay it."

As he leans down to kiss me, Luke and Jake start making kissing noises. Seb looks at them.

"You're excused," he says as he finds my lips again.

"Yes, sir!" They both back up quickly.

"If Sophie ever disappoints you in any way," Jake says, stopping for a second, "please let us know and we will correct it immediately."

"Go away," Seb growls. "Now."

I laugh as my brothers run back into the ballroom.

"That's the most romantic thing anyone has ever done for me," I say as Seb leans over to kiss me again.

"If that's the most romantic thing anyone has done for you, we've got a lot of work to do." He laces his fingers through mine and pulls me back into the ballroom. "Let's start with you teaching me how to dance."

"What? Really? You're going to dance?"

"I'm going to try," he says as he pulls me onto the dance

floor and then turns to face me. "Tell me what to do."

"Well, it's a little like catching," I say, beaming up at him. "First, put your arms around me and trap me to your chest."

He grabs me and pulls me firmly against him. "Done. I like that part. What's next?"

"Just start swaying, kind of like this. Yes, that's perfect!"

"This is where it gets complicated." His forehead wrinkles up. "Do I have to move my feet? I don't want to step on your toes."

"You don't have to, but if you do, I promise I'll keep my feet out of your way."

He moves his feet a little bit side-to-side.

"That's good. And, unlike catching, you can close your eyes if you want."

"I don't want to close my eyes." He smiles down at me. "I like looking at you."

"Mmm," I say, resting my head on his chest.

"Do I have to spin you or anything?"

"No, that would require me moving off your chest and I don't want to do that."

"Yeah, I don't want you to do that either," he says, his hands sinking down my body until they land on my butt.

I open my eyes for a second and see a bunch of phones pointed toward us. I flip my head to the other side. There are just as many phones on this side. They're surrounding us.

"You weren't kidding about the phones being in your face all the time. Do you ever get used to all of the people?"

"What people, baby?" he whispers. "What people?"

Epilogue

SOPHIE

Six Months Later

"Hell no!" I point at the tequila bottle that the waiter just placed right in front of me. "Get that thing off this table."

"Aww, Soph," Savannah laughs. "This is the first time we've all been together since Maisie's wedding."

We're at the same bar where I met Seb six months ago. I haven't been back here since then, but I have spent almost every second with Seb. We haven't been apart for one night since Maisie's wedding. We spent most of the off-season at his family's lake house in Michigan, and then spent a few weeks in The Keys before spring training started. When we finally got back to Miami, he asked me to move in with him. We had my stuff moved into his house in less than twenty-four hours.

"No." I scoot my chair back from the table and point at the

tequila bottle. "Absolutely not. We had a deal last time. Never again."

"Well, I mean, you met Seb the last time we played." Maisie tilts her head and smiles at me. "So maybe this game is good luck."

"Yeah, and I barely remember anything I said to him that night," I say. "You can't play the bride card anymore. I will leave this bar before I play this stupid game again."

"Maybe just one round," Maisie says, taking my hand and smiling way too broadly at me. She's up to something. "There's just one person I want you to tell the truth to—"

"Who? Seb?" I look around the table. Everyone's giggling. "I haven't told any of you one bad thing about him."

"I know, sweetie, not one bad thing." Maisie squeezes my hand as she nods her head at something behind me. "Maybe you should tell him that."

"What?" I turn around to see Seb right behind me—on one knee.

"Hey, Soph," he says, smiling. "Not one bad thing, huh?"

I shake my head as my eyes start to well up. I can't think of anything to say. Since we've been dating, he's taken my breath away a lot. His words, his gestures, his love—they all leave me speechless.

He's gazing at me—his beautiful eyes glowing. He reaches out to hold my hands. "I saw you for the first time in front of this hotel, and I knew when you rolled your eyes at me that I had to get to know you. These last six months—getting to know everything about you—have been the happiest days of my life. I've wanted to ask you this for months, but I've been trying to be patient. I can't anymore. I can't wait. I don't want to spend one more day not knowing if you'll be my wife. I love you, Sophie. Will you please marry me?"

I nod as tears start rolling down my face.

"Can I hear you say it?" He grins as he squeezes my hands.

"Yes," I whisper. "So much yes."

He grabs me into a hug and twirls me around a few times. Everyone in the bar is clapping and stomping their feet.

"Seb! Congratulations, Seb!" The crowd's yelling at us. It happens everywhere we go. I haven't gotten used to it yet, but when Seb hugs me, it all fades into the background.

He puts me down and kisses me. Maisie comes sailing around the table and almost knocks me over as she throws herself into me for a hug.

"Congratulations, honey," she whispers. "You're perfect together. I'm so happy for you."

As Seb pulls me into another hug, I see my friends' husbands descending on the table, followed by Roman and Michael who sandwich Seb and me between them for a group hug.

"Congratulations, Soph," Roman says. "There are only a few people who would even come close to deserving you. I think Seb is one of them."

As the waiter starts pouring champagne around the table, Seb pulls me onto his lap and kisses me again. His hands start sliding down my back.

"There are rooms upstairs if this is the direction it's headed," Roman laughs from beside me. He slaps the back of Seb's head. "Let her come up for air, Seb."

"Fine," Seb growls.

"So, is there a ring?" Savannah yells at Seb from across the table. "I mean you're a gazillionaire. Please tell me you didn't cheap out."

Seb looks at her and shakes his head. He grabs the tequila bottle, pours himself a shot, downs it, and points at her. "Savannah, you're obnoxious. There. I've wanted to tell you that since I met you. Settle down. Learn to have a filter."

Everyone bursts out laughing—even Savannah's husband.

"Um," Serena says. "You're not playing Truth or Tequila correctly. It's either tell the truth or drink. Not both."

"If I'm going to be a permanent part of this group," Seb says, pulling me against his chest, "there are going to be new rules. If we're going to play this game, I'm going to drink and tell anyone what I want them to hear—simultaneously."

"Oh my God, Seb," Taylor says, grabbing the tequila and drinking right out of the bottle. "I love you. There's a truth for you. Welcome to the family."

Seb reaches into his pocket and pulls out a ring box. "I was going to do this later, but since your friends are insisting—"

"Damn right, we're insisting," Michael says. "Let's see the hardware."

Seb blocks everyone's view with his back as he pops open the box. "Again, will you marry me?"

"Seb," I say, gasping as he opens it.

"Is that a yes?" He smiles as he slides it onto my finger.

Maisie runs around the table and grabs my hand. "Holy crap, Seb. People are going to be able to see this ring from space."

"Good. I want everyone to know that she's taken—including the aliens."

"Oh my God," Savannah says as I hold up my left hand. "That's just obnoxious—"

"Savannah!" Seb points at her. "What did I just say? If you're coming after Sophie, you're coming after me. I'm her first line of defense from now on."

"I call second," Roman says. "And I slip into first if Seb isn't around."

"I'm always going to be around," Seb says, giving Roman a fist bump, "but I appreciate the backup, man."

"Your little male bonding is so adorable," Michael says, "but everyone knows that the real first line is Maisie and me. If anyone comes after Sophie, we will bitch slap them into tomorrow. Am I right, Maisie?"

"Girl!" Maisie air high fives him from across the table. "Everyone knows it!"

"Is it possible to get a little alone time?" I whisper into Seb's ear as I circle my arms around his neck.

"Let's just stay in a hug. Maybe everyone will go away."

"Mmm. That sounds amazing." I nuzzle into his neck. "So how long have you had the ring?"

"A couple of months, but I knew I wanted to ask you the day after Maisie's wedding. Do you remember that morning? We stayed in bed until noon watching Disney movies?"

"Yeah, I remember," I say, laying my head on his shoulder. "I started falling in love with you that morning."

"It was about time you caught up," he whispers. "I think I started falling in love with you that first night when I tucked you into bed at this hotel. I knew I needed to give you time, though. Did I give you enough?"

I nod against his shoulder. "Yeah. You could have asked

me about a month into our time in Michigan and I would have said yes."

"Damn," he says, kissing the top of my head. "You would think a catcher would be better at reading signals. I wish I wouldn't have waited this long."

"Make it up to me by having a short engagement," I say, lifting my head off his shoulder. "I want to get married right after your season's over—at the lake house. Small wedding. Only immediate family and close friends."

"Whatever you want, baby," he says, pulling me in for another kiss. "For the rest of your life, whatever you want is yours."

Epilogue

SOPHIE

First chapter of the third book in The Grand Slam Series:
Leave It On The Field

One and Half Years Later
Sophie

"Seb! Stop. Joe will be here in fifteen minutes."

"Thirty," Seb says as he backs me up against the kitchen island. "We have plenty of time."

I grab his hands as they start pulling up my dress. "You know he's always at least fifteen minutes early."

"Okay, he'll be here in fifteen," he says as his face plunges into my neck. "Like I said—plenty of time."

"Stop." My body arches into him like it always does when

he gets anywhere near my neck. "You know the neck thing makes me crazy."

"Really?" He starts nibbling. "I had no idea."

"You did too," I say, running my hands down his back. They land on his butt. "And stop flexing. You know how I feel about your butt muscles."

"They like you too," he whispers as he continues to flex underneath my hands. He knows exactly what to do to put me in the mood. Honestly, it doesn't take that much. Just looking at him does it for me most of the time.

I unzip his jeans and pull him out. Hard again. "We already had sex last night *and* this morning."

His hands dart under my dress. "Not even close to our record for a twenty four hour period."

"I swear you have more than two hands." I sigh as I feel my body pass the point of no return. "And you're way hornier than usual."

"Incorrect. I'm always this exact same amount of horny." He lifts me onto the island.

"Not here," I say, trying to get down. "I'm entertaining later."

"We've had sex on every surface of this house including this one. We can clean it."

He continues the neck work as he pulls my legs around his waist. He fingers me a little before he slides inside. I let out an extended moan as he fills me up.

"That's better," he whispers. "I knew you would come around to my way of thinking, eventually."

I wrap my arms around his neck as he starts pumping. I know it will happen like it always does. The tingling starts in my toes and shoots up my legs. Then my entire body starts shaking. It's such an intense sensation that sometimes it's all I can do not to pass out.

The intercom beeps to announce that security has cleared someone through the gate. "Joe Porter," the voice announces.

"Seb." I groan as he starts panting against my neck. "He's here."

"Take your time." He slides his hands under my butt and picks me up. "He's not getting in until I let him in."

He pushes me against the wall. The shelves to the left of my head start shaking. I think something falls off. My head drops to his shoulder as he whispers something to me. I can't hear him. The roar has started in my brain like it does just before I'm about to lose control.

I hear a knock on the door just as my body releases. I bury my mouth against Seb's neck to try to deaden the long series of sounds pouring out of my mouth. He pumps hard a few more times before he erupts inside of me with a loud grunt that rattles around inside my head as I collapse against him.

He pants into my hair for a few seconds, then whispers, "You had perfect timing, as usual."

"I'm not sure I should get much credit for the timing." I shiver as the sensations continue to tingle through my body. "You know I pretty much lose control once you're inside."

"Really?" He wraps me up tighter. "I had no idea."

"You're such a liar. I really horny liar," I say, laughing as I rub my head against his chest to try to get it to stop spinning. "Joe's waiting."

"He can wait." He kisses the top of my head as he starts rubbing my back. "You need your recovery time."

"Since it usually takes me about an hour to recover from all that, you might as well let him in now."

He presses me more firmly against the wall as his tongue parts my lips. My head starts spinning again as he takes a slow, deep kiss.

"Stop," I say when he finally pulls back. "That doesn't help my recovery."

He brushes his cheek against mine. "I'm going to miss you so much."

"It's only a couple days," I say, running my fingers through his hair.

"It shouldn't be any days. I've played for this team for nine seasons. They've never made us stay in a hotel before home games."

"This is your first World Series. I guess they think it's different."

Another knock at the door. Well, really more like a pounding.

He carries me over to the intercom. "Be there in a minute, Joe."

"Yep," Joe gets out before Seb clicks it off.

He sets me back down on the island and nuzzles his face into my hair as I start to unwind myself from his body. "You're everything to me. I'd quit baseball today if you wanted me to. You know that, right? If this all gets to be too much for you, just tell me and I'm done that second."

"It's not too much. I don't want you to quit." I nod toward the front door. "You need to let him in before he breaks down the door. Go."

He brushes his lips over mine, sighs, and then heads toward the front door.

"What took you so long?" Joe's gruff tone vibrates through the house. "We're already running late."

"Do we really have to do this?" Seb asks as he walks back into the kitchen. "It's bullshit."

"Hey, Soph." Joe follows Seb around the corner. "You ready for this week?"

"Hey, Joe." I glance up at him as I'm picking up the book that fell off the shelf. "Yeah, I think. It's going to be crazy."

Seb pulls me back against him. "It would be less crazy if the team would let us stay with our wives like we're grown-ass men."

"I'll be fine," I say as he circles his arms around me. "Really. Just worry about baseball for the next few weeks."

Joe points toward the front door. "Seb, we need to leave. Drew said everyone had to be in the hotel by two. It's 1:28. With traffic, we'll be lucky to even make it on time at this point."

Seb doesn't move. "I play better when I spend the night before a game with my wife."

"Why are you arguing with me?" Joe throws up his hands. "You know it's not my decision. I'm paid to get you where you need to go safely. And right now, where you need to go is that fucking hotel."

"Babe, you have to go." I take Seb's hand and pull him toward the foyer. He follows me, dragging his feet. "I'll see you at the party tonight."

"For what? Like twenty minutes?" He picks up his suitcase as Joe opens the front door.

"Babe," I say, squeezing his hand, "it's not like we'd be alone here anyway. Our parents are arriving in the next few hours. And your sister and my brothers come in tomorrow. Our house will be packed."

"I'm here!" Maisie bursts through the front door. Joe grabs her and pushes her against a wall. She screeches. "Jesus, Joe! It's me. Lighten up."

"Have you ever heard of knocking?" Joe releases her slowly. "Don't surprise me. You know I hate that. How did you even get in here? Security didn't call to clear you."

"The door was open. And I'm on the no-ring list. You know how much Sophie hates that intercom going off." Maisie pats his back. "You really need to settle down. I mean, you're hyper most of the time but the World Series is going to kill you."

"Sophie," Joe says, narrowing his eyes, "what did I tell you about the no-ring list? The more people you put on it, the more confusing it gets for the guards. They make more mistakes as the list grows longer. I don't want anyone surprising you—not even your best friend."

"Maisie's the only person I've added," I say, pulling her away from Joe and hugging her to my chest. "But yes, this is a surprise. What are you doing here?"

"What do you mean?" She looks at Seb who's trying to subtly shake his head at her. "Seb asked me to come over and hang with you until his parents get here."

"Seb." I look back at him—my eyebrows raised. "Really? I don't need a babysitter."

"I'm your husband. I get to be worried." He puts his suit-case back down. "Too many people are talking about you right now. The social media stuff has gotten out of hand. That one bitch said she would kill you—"

"It's a figure of speech," I say. "She didn't mean it literally."

"Joe," Seb says, "has she posted anything since this morning?"

"No. And I agree with Sophie. It's just smack talk. You should be used to it by now."

"I'm used to it for me, not for Sophie." Seb pulls me back over to him. "I'm going to lose it if people don't stop talking about her."

"Babe," I say, rubbing my forehead against his chest. For some reason that usually calms him down. "It's gotten so much better since I deleted my accounts. I don't even look at it unless you show me."

"Seb." Joe points toward the door again. "Now. Let's go."

"Okay." Seb's voice is as tense as his body.

"I'll be fine," I say, looking up at him. "I'll see you tonight."

"I wish you would let me hire a bodyguard—"

"Seb, no. We talked about that. I don't want a stranger following me around." I nod back at Maisie. "She can be my bodyguard."

He grunts. "Well it's better than you being alone. Mae, will you stay until my parents get here?"

"I'm not leaving her side. And who's going to get to her in this house? It's on an island with only one way in."

"No one monitors the bay," Seb says. "They could come off the water."

"Your security system—including on the bay side—is

almost better than what they have at the White House," Joe says. "All we're missing is Secret Service agents."

"Okay." Seb takes a deep breath and slowly exhales. "Soph, remember to text me when you leave for the hotel."

"I will. Go. You're playing in your first World Series. I'm so proud of you, baby. Promise me you'll enjoy every minute of it."

He nods and finally smiles. "I promise, but just for you. Come on, Joe. Hurry up. We're late."

"Unbelievable," Joe says as he watches Seb walk out of the door. He turns to me. "I'm going to kill him by the end of this."

"You're a saint, Joe." I pat his shoulder. "Not many people could deal with him when he gets this way."

I close the door and turn back to Maisie. "Good Lord. I didn't think Seb would leave. He's been pacing around all morning."

"He's worried about you." She takes my hand and pulls me into the kitchen. "I didn't think he would recover after that guy grabbed your ass at the game in June."

"The only reason he recovered is because I agreed to sit in the owner's suite for games now. There's no way he could concentrate if I was still sitting in the stands." I take a bottle of wine out of the refrigerator. "Too early?"

"Never. What time are you leaving for the sponsor party tonight?"

"I need to get there around six to help Dottie prep her speech."

"I'm still confused." Her forehead crinkles up. "Are you officially working for the team again?"

"No, but this is Dottie's first year owning a team and she's already hosting a World Series." I give the island an extra wipe down before I place a charcuterie plate between us. "She's freaked out. I told her I would help her through the postseason."

"Dot seems like a tough old broad. I can't believe she's letting this rattle her."

"She is tough, but I think since her husband died, she feels more exposed. You know? She doesn't have that backup."

Maisie grabs a piece of cheese. "Well, I hope she doesn't die for a while. Seb seems to like her."

"*Loves* her. The entire team does. She's so sweet. She's like a grandma to them. I was going to tell her no when she asked me to help out in the postseason. Seb talked me into it just so Dottie would feel more secure."

She sticks out her tongue as she takes a bite of the Limburger. "This tastes like butt."

"It's Seb's dad's favorite," I say, handing her a napkin. "It smells awful."

She spits out the cheese and rinses the bad taste out with a swig of wine. "We're sitting in a suite for the games, right?"

"Yeah, it's so much easier than buying individual tickets for everyone. With our family and friends, we have twenty-seven people, and that's after cutting the list several times."

She drains her wine glass. "Don't players get free tickets?"

"Only six for postseason games. Seb's are right behind the dugout. He's giving them to his parents, his high school coach, and his Michigan friends. They've been with him from day one. He said they deserve those seats more than anyone."

She smiles. "That Seb is just a good guy."

"Yes, he is. He's the best guy."

Maisie jumps when the security booth intercom beeps. "God, I don't know how you've gotten used to that thing. It's so loud."

I shrug as I answer it. "Hey, this is Sophie."

"Hey, Mrs. Miller. It's Steve. Seb's parents are at the gate. They're on the permanent clear list, but they wanted me to call you before they came in."

"Thanks, Steve. Send them up."

"Done. They're headed your way."

"You drink way too slowly," Maisie says as she grabs my wine, drains it, and then puts our empty wine glasses into the dishwasher. "Hide the evidence. I don't want your in-laws to think you're a drunk."

"They both drink way more than I do. His mom always thinks I'm pregnant when I turn down alcohol. She can't accept that I'm just a lightweight."

"She hopes you're pregnant," Maisie says, rolling her eyes. "I've been married longer than you, but I don't have near the amount of pressure you have to reproduce."

"Right? And it's from all sides. Everyone wants the heir to the great Seb Miller to be born."

"Except for the great Seb Miller," she says as we head toward the front door. "Does he still want to wait?"

"Yeah, and I get it. He wants to spend as much time as possible with our kids. He can't do that while he's playing. I'm ready now, but we're waiting. We're trying to time it with his retirement in a few years."

I open the door just in time to see the Millers turning into

our driveway. Seb's mom, Adie, has her arm out the window
—waving at us.

"I'm leaving," Maisie says, hugging me. "I can't take too
much of Adie's enthusiasm until I've had more to drink. I'll
see you at the game tomorrow night."

Buy or download Leave it on the Field on Amazon.

What's next?

Seb and Sophie are back in the second and third books of The Grand Slam Series. Raine Out and Leave It On The Field are available on Amazon.

The second book of The Grand Slam Series takes place at Seb and Sophie's wedding. *Raine Out* is the story of Sophie's friend, Raine, searching for love with Seb's teammate, Alex.

A steamy romantic comedy. It's all fun and games until someone catches feelings. A driven career woman who has no time for love. A professional baseball player who has no desire for commitment. But when they come together for their friends' island wedding, the mesmerizing beach breezes have them wanting to find time for each other—if only for one steamy weekend.

Raine

I haven't spent much time with Sophie since we were kids. When we started high school, we headed in different directions and never looked back. She invited me to her wedding this weekend. I don't want to go because despite all our years apart, I know one thing hasn't changed: her mission to find me the perfect man. I've told her I don't have time for dating, but she never listens. I'm guessing she's going to be pushing some guy at me the minute I get off the plane.

Alex

My teammate Seb's getting married this weekend. I'm happy for him, but I can't relate to it at all. He wants to spend the rest of his life with Sophie. I don't even want to spend the rest of the night with the women who end up in my bed. I'm fine with that, but for some reason, Sophie's not. Even with my best efforts to stop it, she's been trying to find me love since the day we met. She told me one of her childhood friends is coming to the wedding, so I'm guessing that's who I'll be hiding from all weekend. Let the games begin.

"Another win! Kickass characters, witty banter, strong female lead and a great story that sucks you in and has you rooting for Raine and Alex before they even meet. Can't wait for the next one in the series!" Amazon Review

"So funny! Butch is the character that I didn't know I needed in my life! This book can definitely be read alone, but you'll love it so much more if you read The Trident Trilogy and Truth or Tequila first." Amazon Review

The third book of The Grand Slam Series, *Leave It On The Field*, takes place a year and a half after *Truth or Tequila* as Seb's team prepares to play in the World Series.

Professional baseball player Seb Miller and his new wife, Sophie, are blissfully happy. Stupidly happy. The kind of happy that makes other people jealous. So jealous in fact, that someone has started coming after Sophie on social media. It wasn't much at first, but as Seb's team heads into the World Series, the posts begin to reveal intimate details about their relationship that only someone very close to them would know.

Sophie

When I met Seb, my life changed completely—mostly for the better. When we're alone, it's magical. He's the most loving, attentive man in the world. Unfortunately part of being married to a famous man is having everyone in your business. It wasn't too bad at first, but now there's someone on social media telling the world about the most private parts of our lives. Everyone's talking about it. And now I can't go anywhere without being recognized. It's exhausting, and honestly, I'm not sure how much longer I can take it.

Seb

For me, the worst part about being a professional athlete is the fame. Hands down. Nothing else even comes close. I'm a quiet guy. I'm even a little bit shy. The attention is overwhelming at times, but I deal with it because it's part of my job description. But now my fame is affecting Sophie. People are starting to harass her. And that can't happen. She's more important to me than anything—baseball included. I've told her I'll quit playing the second she tells me it's too much— that very second. Even if it's in the middle of the World Series.

All of my books are available on Amazon.

Go to donnaschwartze.com for a suggested reading order. While you're there, sign up for my email newsletter to be the first to know when I publish new books.

About the Author

Donna Schwartze is a graduate of the University of Missouri School of Journalism. She also holds a Master of Arts from Webster University. She is an avid yogi and plans to still be able to do the splits on her 100th birthday. Her favorite character from her books is Mack from The Trident Trilogy.

Made in the USA
Las Vegas, NV
22 November 2022

59862607R00166